PENGUIN BOOKS

THE HAUNTING

Shirley Jackson was born in San Francisco in 1916. She first received wide critical acclaim for her short story "The Lottery," which was published in 1949. Her novels—which also include *The Sundial, The Bird's Nest, Hangsaman, The Road through the Wall,* and *We Have Always Lived in the Castle* (Penguin)— are characterized by her use of realistic settings for tales that often involve elements of horror and the occult. *Raising Demons* and *Life Among the Savages* (Penguin) are her two works of nonfiction. *Come Along With Me* (Penguin) is a collection of stories, lectures, and part of the novel she was working on when she died in 1965.

SHIRLEY JACKSON

———

THE HAUNTING

PENGUIN BOOKS

PENGUIN BOOKS

Published by the Penguin Group
Penguin Putnam Inc., 375 Hudson Street,
New York, New York 10014, U.S.A.
Penguin Books Ltd, 27 Wrights Lane,
London W8 5TZ, England
Penguin Books Australia Ltd, Ringwood,
Victoria, Australia
Penguin Books Canada Ltd, 10 Alcorn Avenue,
Toronto, Ontario, Canada M4V 3B2
Penguin Books (N.Z.) Ltd, 182–190 Wairau Road,
Auckland 10, New Zealand

Penguin Books Ltd, Registered Offices:
Harmondsworth, Middlesex, England

First published in the United States of America as
The Haunting of Hill House by The Viking Press 1959
First published in Canada by The Macmillan Company of Canada Limited 1959
Published in Penguin Books 1984
This edition with the title *The Haunting* published in Penguin Books 1999

10 9 8 7 6 5 4 3 2 1

ISBN 0 14 02.8743 4
(CIP data available)

Printed in the United States of America
Set in Janson

For LEONARD BROWN

THE HAUNTING

~~~~~~

NO LIVE organism can continue for long to exist sanely under conditions of absolute reality; even larks and katydids are supposed, by some, to dream. Hill House, not sane, stood by itself against its hills, holding darkness within; it had stood so for eighty years and might stand for eighty more. Within, walls continued upright, bricks met neatly, floors were firm, and doors were sensibly shut; silence lay steadily against the wood and stone of Hill House, and whatever walked there, walked alone.

Dr. John Montague was a doctor of philosophy; he had taken his degree in anthropology, feeling obscurely that in this field he might come closest to his true vocation, the analysis of supernatural manifestations. He was scrupulous about the use of his title because, his investigations being so utterly unscientific, he hoped to borrow an air of respectability, even scholarly authority, from his education. It had cost him a good deal, in money and pride, since he was not a begging man, to rent Hill House for three months, but he expected absolutely to be compensated for his pains by the sensation following upon the publication of his definitive work on the causes and effects of psychic disturbances in a house commonly known as "haunted." He had been looking for an honestly haunted house all his life. When he heard of Hill House he had been at first doubtful, then hopeful, then indefatigable; he was not the man to let go of Hill House once he had found it.

Dr. Montague's intentions with regard to Hill House derived from the methods of the intrepid nineteenth-century ghost hunters; he was going to go and live in Hill House and see what happened there. It was his intention, at first, to follow the example of the anonymous Lady who went to stay at Ballechin House and ran a summer-long house party for skeptics and believers, with croquet and ghost-watching as the outstanding attractions, but skeptics, believers, and good croquet players are harder to come by today; Dr. Montague was forced to engage assistants. Perhaps the leisurely ways of Victorian life lent themselves more agreeably to the devices of psychic investigation, or perhaps the painstaking documentation of phenomena has largely gone out as a means of determining actuality; at any rate, Dr. Montague had not only to engage assistants but to search for them.

Because he thought of himself as careful and conscientious, he spent considerable time looking for his assistants. He combed the records of the psychic societies, the back files of sensational newspapers, the reports of parapsychologists, and assembled a list of names of people who had, in one way or another, at one time or another, no matter how briefly or dubiously, been involved in abnormal events. From his list he first eliminated the names of people who were dead. When he had then crossed off the names of those who seemed to him publicity-seekers, of subnormal intelligence, or unsuitable because of a clear tendency to take the center of the stage, he had a list of perhaps a dozen names. Each of these people, then, received a letter from Dr. Montague extending an invitation to spend all or part of a summer at a comfortable country house, old, but perfectly equipped with plumbing, electricity, central heating, and clean mattresses. The purpose of their stay, the letters stated clearly, was to observe and explore the various unsavory stories which had been circulated about the house for most of its eighty years of existence. Dr. Montague's letters did not say openly that Hill House was haunted, because Dr. Montague was a man of science and until he had actually experienced a psychic manifestation in Hill House he would not trust his luck too far. Consequently his letters had a certain ambiguous dignity calculated to catch at the imagination of a very special sort of reader. To his dozen letters, Dr. Montague had four replies, the other eight or so candidates having presumably moved and left no forwarding address, or possibly having lost interest in the supernormal, or even, perhaps, never having existed at all. To the four who replied, Dr. Montague wrote again, naming a specific day when the house would be officially regarded as ready for occupancy, and enclosing detailed directions for reaching it, since, as he was forced to explain, information about finding the house was extremely difficult to get, particularly from the rural community which surrounded it. On the day before he was to leave for Hill House, Dr. Montague was persuaded to take into his select company a representative of the family who owned the house, and a telegram arrived from one of his candidates, backing out with a clearly manufactured excuse. Another never came or wrote, perhaps because of some pressing personal problem which had intervened. The other two came.

2

Eleanor Vance was thirty-two years old when she came to Hill House. The only person in the world she genuinely hated, now that her mother was dead, was her sister. She disliked her brother-in-law and her five-year-old niece, and she had no friends. This was owing largely to the eleven years she had spent caring for her invalid mother, which had left her with some proficiency as a nurse and an inability to face strong sunlight without blinking. She could not remember ever being truly happy in her adult life; her years with her mother had been built up devotedly around small guilts and small reproaches, constant weariness, and unending despair. Without ever wanting to become reserved and shy, she had spent so long alone, with no one to love, that it was difficult for her to talk, even casually, to another person without self-consciousness and an awkward inability to find words. Her name had turned up on Dr. Montague's list because one day, when she was twelve years old and her sister was eighteen, and their father had been dead for not quite a month, showers of stones had fallen on their house, without any warning or any indication of purpose or reason, dropping from the ceilings, rolling loudly down the walls, breaking windows and pattering maddeningly on the roof. The stones continued intermittently for three days, during which time Eleanor and her sister were less unnerved by the stones than by the neighbors and sight-seers who gathered daily outside the front door, and by their mother's blind, hysterical insistence that all of this was due to malicious, backbiting people on the block who had had it in for her ever since she came. After three days Eleanor and her sister were removed to the house of a friend, and the stones stopped falling, nor did they ever return, although Eleanor and her sister and her mother went back to living in the house, and the feud with the entire neighborhood was never ended. The story had been forgotten by everyone except the people Dr. Montague consulted; it had certainly been forgotten by Eleanor and her sister, each of whom had supposed at the time that the other was responsible.

During the whole underside of her life, ever since her first memory, Eleanor had been waiting for something like Hill House. Caring for her mother, lifting a cross old lady from her chair to her bed, setting out endless little trays of soup and oatmeal, steeling herself to the filthy laundry, Eleanor had held fast to the belief that someday something would happen. She had accepted the invitation to Hill House by return mail, although her brother-in-law had insisted upon calling a couple of people to make sure that this doctor fellow was not aiming to introduce Eleanor to savage rites not unconnected with matters Eleanor's sister deemed it improper for an unmarried young woman to know. Perhaps, Eleanor's sister whispered in the privacy of the marital bedroom, perhaps Dr. Montague—if that really *was* his name, after all—perhaps this Dr. Montague *used* these women for some—well—*experiments*. *You* know —*experiments*, the way they do. Eleanor's sister dwelt richly upon experiments she had heard these doctors did. Eleanor had no such ideas, or, having them, was not afraid. Eleanor, in short, would have gone anywhere.

Theodora—that was as much name as she used; her sketches were signed "Theo" and on her apartment door and the window of her shop and her telephone listing and her pale stationery and the bottom of the lovely photograph of her which stood on the mantel, the name was always only Theodora—Theodora was not at all like Eleanor. Duty and conscience were, for Theodora, attributes which belonged properly to Girl Scouts. Theodora's world was one of delight and soft colors; she had come onto Dr. Montague's list because—going laughing into the laboratory, bringing with her a rush of floral perfume—she had somehow been able, amused and excited over her own incredible skill, to identify correctly eighteen cards out of twenty, fifteen cards out of twenty, nineteen cards out of twenty, held up by an assistant out of sight and hearing. The name of Theodora shone in the records of the laboratory and so came inevitably to Dr. Montague's attention. Theodora had been entertained by Dr. Montague's first letter and answered it out of curiosity (perhaps the wakened knowledge in Theodora which told her the names of symbols on cards held out of sight urged her on her way toward Hill House), and yet fully intended to decline the invitation. Yet—perhaps the stirring, urgent sense again— when Dr. Montague's confirming letter arrived, Theodora had been tempted and had somehow plunged blindly, wantonly, into a violent quarrel with the friend with whom she shared an apartment. Things were said on both sides which only time could eradicate; Theodora had deliberately and heartlessly smashed the lovely little figurine her friend had carved of her, and her friend had cruelly ripped to shreds the volume of Alfred de Musset which had been a birthday present from Theodora, taking particular pains with the page which bore Theodora's loving, teasing inscription. These acts were of course unforgettable, and before they could laugh over them together time would have to go by; Theodora had written that night, accepting Dr. Montague's invitation, and departed in cold silence the next day.

Luke Sanderson was a liar. He was also a thief. His aunt, who was the owner of Hill House, was fond of pointing out that her nephew had the best education, the best clothes, the best taste, and the worst companions of anyone she had ever known; she would have leaped at any chance to put him safely away for a few weeks. The family lawyer was prevailed upon to persuade Dr. Montague that the house could on no account be rented to him for his pur-

poses without the confining presence of a member of the
family during his stay, and perhaps at their first meeting
the doctor perceived in Luke a kind of strength, or catlike
instinct for self-preservation, which made him almost as
anxious as Mrs. Sanderson to have Luke with him in the
house. At any rate, Luke was amused, his aunt grateful,
and Dr. Montague more than satisfied. Mrs. Sanderson told
the family lawyer that at any rate there was really nothing
in the house Luke could steal. The old silver there was of
some value, she told the lawyer, but it represented an almost insuperable difficulty for Luke: it required energy to
steal it and transform it into money. Mrs. Sanderson did
Luke an injustice. Luke was not at all likely to make off
with the family silver, or Dr. Montague's watch, or Theodora's bracelet; his dishonesty was largely confined to taking petty cash from his aunt's pocketbook and cheating at
cards. He was also apt to sell the watches and cigarette
cases given him, fondly and with pretty blushes, by his
aunt's friends. Someday Luke would inherit Hill House,
but he had never thought to find himself living in it.

3

"I just don't think she should take the car, is all,"
Eleanor's brother-in-law said stubbornly.

"It's half my car," Eleanor said. "I helped pay for it."

"I just don't think she should take it, is all," her brother-
in-law said. He appealed to his wife. "It isn't fair she should
have the use of it for the whole summer, and us have to do
without."

"Carrie drives it all the time, and I never even take it out
of the garage," Eleanor said. "Besides, you'll be in the

mountains all summer, and you can't use it *there*. Carrie, you know you won't use the car in the mountains."

"But suppose poor little Linnie got sick or something? And we needed a car to get her to a doctor?"

"It's half my car," Eleanor said. "I mean to take it."

"Suppose even *Carrie* got sick? Suppose we couldn't get a doctor and needed to go to a hospital?"

"I want it. I mean to take it."

"I don't think so." Carrie spoke slowly, deliberately. "We don't know where you're going, do we? You haven't seen fit to tell us very much about all this, have you? I don't think I can see my way clear to letting you borrow my car."

"It's half my car."

"No," Carrie said. "You may not."

"Right." Eleanor's brother-in-law nodded. "We need it, like Carrie says."

Carrie smiled slightly. "I'd never forgive myself, Eleanor, if I lent you the car and something happened. How do we know we can trust this doctor fellow? You're still a young woman, after all, and the car is worth a good deal of money."

"Well, now, Carrie, I *did* call Homer in the credit office, and he said this fellow was in good standing at some college or other—"

Carrie said, still smiling, "Of course, there is *every* reason to suppose that he is a decent man. But Eleanor does not choose to tell us where she is going, or how to reach her if we want the car back; something could happen, and we might never know. Even if Eleanor," she went on delicately, addressing her teacup, "even if *Eleanor* is prepared to run off to the ends of the earth at the invitation of any man, there is *still* no reason why she should be permitted to take my car with her."

"It's half my car."

"Suppose poor little Linnie got sick, up there in the mountains, with nobody around? No doctor?"

"In any case, Eleanor, I am sure that I am doing what Mother would have thought best. Mother had confidence in me and would certainly never have approved my letting you run wild, going off heaven knows where, in my car."

"Or suppose even *I* got sick, up there in—"

"I am sure Mother would have agreed with me, Eleanor."

"Besides," Eleanor's brother-in-law said, struck by a sudden idea, "how do we know she'd bring it back in good condition?"

There has to be a first time for everything, Eleanor told herself. She got out of the taxi, very early in the morning, trembling because by now, perhaps, her sister and her brother-in-law might be stirring with the first faint proddings of suspicion; she took her suitcase quickly out of the taxi while the driver lifted out the cardboard carton which had been on the front seat. Eleanor overtipped him, wondering if her sister and brother-in-law were following, were perhaps even now turning into the street and telling each other, "There she is, just as we thought, the thief, there she is"; she turned in haste to go into the huge city garage where their car was kept, glancing nervously toward the ends of the street. She crashed into a very little lady, sending packages in all directions, and saw with dismay a bag upset and break on the sidewalk, spilling out a broken piece of cheesecake, tomato slices, a hard roll. "Damn you damn you!" the little lady screamed, her face pushed up close to Eleanor's. "I was taking it home, damn you damn you!"

"I'm so sorry," Eleanor said; she bent down, but it did not seem possible to scoop up the fragments of tomato and cheesecake and shove them somehow back into the broken bag. The old lady was scowling down and snatching up her other packages before Eleanor could reach them, and at last Eleanor rose, smiling in convulsive apology. "I'm really so sorry," she said.

"Damn you," the little old lady said, but more quietly. "I was taking it home for my little lunch. And now, thanks to *you*—"

"Perhaps I could pay?" Eleanor took hold of her pocketbook, and the little lady stood very still and thought.

"I couldn't take money, just like that," she said at last. "I didn't buy the things, you see. They were left over." She snapped her lips angrily. "You should have seen the ham they had," she said, "but someone *else* got *that*. And the chocolate cake. And the potato salad. And the little candies in the little paper dishes. I was too late on *every*thing. And now . . ." She and Eleanor both glanced down at the mess on the sidewalk, and the little lady said, "So you see, I couldn't just take money, not money just from your hand, not for something that was left over."

"May I buy you something to replace this, then? I'm in a terrible hurry, but if we could find some place that's open—"

The little old lady smiled wickedly. "I've still got *this*, anyway," she said, and she hugged one package tight. "You may pay my taxi fare home," she said. "Then no one *else* will be likely to knock me down."

"Gladly," Eleanor said and turned to the taxi driver, who had been waiting, interested. "Can you take this lady home?" she asked.

"A couple of dollars will do it," the little lady said, "not including the tip for this gentleman, of course. Being as small as *I* am," she explained daintily, "it's quite a hazard, quite a hazard indeed, people knocking you down. Still, it's a genuine pleasure to find one as willing as you to make up for it. Sometimes the people who knock you down never turn once to look." With Eleanor's help she climbed into the taxi with her packages, and Eleanor took two dollars and a fifty-cent piece from her pocketbook and handed them to the little lady, who clutched them tight in her tiny hand.

"All right, sweetheart," the taxi driver said, "where do we go?"

The little lady chuckled. "I'll tell you after we start," she said, and then, to Eleanor, "Good luck to you, dearie. Watch out from now on how you go knocking people down."

"Good-by," Eleanor said, "and I'm really very sorry."

"That's fine, then," the little lady said, waving at her as the taxi pulled away from the curb. "I'll be praying for you, dearie."

Well, Eleanor thought, staring after the taxi, there's one person, anyway, who will be praying for me. One person anyway.

4

It was the first genuinely shining day of summer, a time of year which brought Eleanor always to aching memories of her early childhood, when it had seemed to be summer all the time; she could not remember a winter before her father's death on a cold wet day. She had taken to wondering lately, during these swift-counted years, what had been done with all those wasted summer days; how could she have spent them so wantonly? I am foolish, she told herself early every summer, I am very foolish; I am grown up now and know the values of things. Nothing is ever really wasted, she believed sensibly, even one's childhood, and then each year, one summer morning, the warm wind would come down the city street where she walked and she would be touched with the little cold thought: I have let more time go by. Yet this morning, driving the little car which she and her sister owned together, apprehensive lest they might still realize that she had come after all and just taken it away, going docilely along the street, following the lines of traffic, stopping when she was bidden and turning when she could, she smiled out at the sunlight slanting along the street and thought, I am going, I am going, I have finally taken a step.

Always before, when she had her sister's permission to drive the little car, she had gone cautiously, moving with extreme care to avoid even the slightest scratch or mar which might irritate her sister, but today, with her carton on the back seat and her suitcase on the floor, her gloves and pocketbook and light coat on the seat beside her, the car belonged entirely to her, a little contained world all her own; I am really going, she thought.

At the last traffic light in the city, before she turned to go onto the great highway out of town, she stopped, waiting, and slid Dr. Montague's letter out of her pocketbook. I will not even need a map, she thought; he must be a very careful man. ". . . Route 39 to Ashton," the letter said, "and then turn left onto Route 5 going west. Follow this for a little less than thirty miles, and you will come to the small village of Hillsdale. Go through Hillsdale to the corner with a gas station on the left and a church on the right, and turn left here onto what seems to be a narrow country road; you will be going up into the hills and the road is very poor. Follow this road to the end—about six miles—and you will come to the gates of Hill House. I am making these directions so detailed because it is inadvisable to stop in Hillsdale to ask your way. The people there are rude to strangers and openly hostile to anyone inquiring about Hill House.

"I am very happy that you will be joining us in Hill House, and will take great pleasure in making your acquaintance on Thursday the twenty-first of June. . . ."

The light changed; she turned onto the highway and was free of the city. No one, she thought, can catch me now; they don't even know which way I'm going.

She had never driven far alone before. The notion of dividing her lovely journey into miles and hours was silly; she saw it, bringing her car with precision between the line on the road and the line of trees beside the road, as a passage of moments, each one new, carrying her along with them, taking her down a path of incredible novelty to a new place. The journey itself was her positive action, her destination vague, unimagined, perhaps nonexistent. She meant to savor each turn of her traveling, loving the road and the trees and the houses and the small ugly towns, teasing herself with the notion that she might take it into her head to stop just anywhere and never leave again. She might pull her car to the side of the highway—although that was not allowed, she told herself; she would be punished if she really did—and leave it behind while she wandered off past the trees into the soft, welcoming country beyond. She might wander till she was exhausted, chasing butterflies or following a stream, and then come at nightfall to the hut of some poor woodcutter who would offer her shelter; she might make her home forever in East Barrington or Desmond or the incorporated village of Berk; she might never leave the road at all, but just hurry on and on until the wheels of the car were worn to nothing and she had come to the end of the world.

And, she thought, I might just go along to Hill House, where I am expected and where I am being given shelter and room and board and a small token salary in consideration of forsaking my commitments and involvements in the city and running away to see the world. I wonder what Dr. Montague is like. I wonder what Hill House is like. I wonder who else will be there.

She was well away from the city now, watching for the turning onto Route 39, that magic thread of road Dr. Montague had chosen for her, out of all the roads in the world, to bring her safely to him and to Hill House; no other road could lead her from where she was to where she wanted to be. Dr. Montague was confirmed, made infallible; under

the sign which pointed the way to Route 39 was another
sign saying: ASHTON, 121 MILES.

The road, her intimate friend now, turned and dipped,
going around turns where surprises waited—once a cow,
regarding her over a fence, once an incurious dog—down
into hollows where small towns lay, past fields and
orchards. On the main street of one village she passed a vast
house, pillared and walled, with shutters over the windows
and a pair of stone lions guarding the steps, and she thought
that perhaps she might live there, dusting the lions each
morning and patting their heads good night. Time is beginning this morning in June, she assured herself, but it is
a time that is strangely new and of itself; in these few sec-
onds I have lived a lifetime in a house with two lions in
front. Every morning I swept the porch and dusted the
lions, and every evening I patted their heads good night,
and once a week I washed their faces and manes and paws
with warm water and soda and cleaned between their teeth
with a swab. Inside the house the rooms were tall and clear
with shining floors and polished windows. A little dainty
old lady took care of me, moving starchily with a silver tea
service on a tray and bringing me a glass of elderberry wine
each evening for my health's sake. I took my dinner alone
in the long, quiet dining room at the gleaming table, and
between the tall windows the white paneling of the walls
shone in the candlelight; I dined upon a bird, and radishes
from the garden, and homemade plum jam. When I slept
it was under a canopy of white organdy, and a nightlight
guarded me from the hall. People bowed to me on the
streets of the town because everyone was very proud of
my lions. When I died . . .

She had left the town far behind by now, and was going past dirty, closed lunch stands and torn signs. There had been a fair somewhere near here once, long ago, with motorcycle races; the signs still carried fragments of words. DARE, one of them read, and another, EVIL, and she laughed at herself, perceiving how she sought out omens everywhere; the word is DAREDEVIL, Eleanor, daredevil drivers, and she slowed her car because she was driving too fast and might reach Hill House too soon.

At one spot she stopped altogether beside the road to stare in disbelief and wonder. Along the road for perhaps a quarter of a mile she had been passing and admiring a row of splendid tended oleanders, blooming pink and white in a steady row. Now she had come to the gateway they protected, and past the gateway the trees continued. The gateway was no more than a pair of ruined stone pillars, with a road leading away between them into empty fields. She could see that the oleander trees cut away from the road and ran up each side of a great square, and she could see all the way to the farther side of the square, which was a line of oleander trees seemingly going along a little river. Inside the oleander square there was nothing, no house, no building, nothing but the straight road going across and ending at the stream. Now what was here, she wondered, what was here and is gone, or what was going to be here and never came? Was it going to be a house or a garden or an orchard; were they driven away forever or are they coming back? Oleanders are poisonous, she remembered; could they be here guarding something? Will I, she thought, will I get out of my car and go between the ruined gates and then, once I am in the magic oleander square, find that I have wandered into a fairyland, protected poisonously from the eyes of people passing? Once I have stepped between the magic gateposts, will I find myself through the protective barrier, the spell broken? I will go into a sweet garden, with fountains and low benches and roses trained over arbors, and find one path—jeweled, perhaps, with rubies and emeralds, soft enough for a king's daughter to walk upon with her little sandaled feet—and it will lead me directly to the palace which lies under a spell. I will walk up low stone steps past stone lions guarding and into a courtyard where a fountain plays and the queen waits, weeping, for the princess to return. She will drop her embroidery when she sees me, and cry out to the palace servants—stirring at last after their long sleep—to prepare a great feast, because the enchantment is ended and the palace is itself again. And we shall live happily ever after.

No, of course, she thought, turning to start her car again, once the palace becomes visible and the spell is broken, the *whole* spell will be broken and all this countryside outside the oleanders will return to its proper form, fading away, towns and signs and cows, into a soft green picture from a fairy tale. Then, coming down from the hills there will be a prince riding, bright in green and silver with a hundred bowmen riding behind him, pennants stirring, horses tossing, jewels flashing . . .

She laughed and turned to smile good-by at the magic oleanders. Another day, she told them, another day I'll come back and break your spell.

She stopped for lunch after she had driven a hundred miles and a mile. She found a country restaurant which advertised itself as an old mill and found herself seated, incredibly, upon a balcony over a dashing stream, looking down upon wet rocks and the intoxicating sparkle of moving water, with a cut-glass bowl of cottage cheese on the table before her, and corn sticks in a napkin. Because this was a time and a land where enchantments were swiftly made and broken she wanted to linger over her lunch, knowing that Hill House always waited for her at the end of her day. The only other people in the dining room were a family party, a mother and father with a small boy and girl, and they talked to one another softly and gently, and once the little girl turned and regarded Eleanor with frank curiosity and, after a minute, smiled. The lights from the stream below touched the ceiling and the polished tables and glanced along the little girl's curls, and the little girl's mother said, "She wants her cup of stars."

Eleanor looked up, surprised; the little girl was sliding back in her chair, sullenly refusing her milk, while her father frowned and her brother giggled and her mother said calmly, "She wants her cup of stars."

Indeed yes, Eleanor thought; indeed, so do I; a cup of stars, of course.

"Her little cup," the mother was explaining, smiling apologetically at the waitress, who was thunderstruck at the thought that the mill's good country milk was not rich enough for the little girl. "It has stars in the bottom, and she always drinks her milk from it at home. She calls it her cup of stars because she can see the stars while she drinks her milk." The waitress nodded, unconvinced, and the mother told the little girl, "You'll have your milk from your cup of stars tonight when we get home. But just for now, just to be a very good little girl, will you take a little milk from this glass?"

Don't do it, Eleanor told the little girl; insist on your cup of stars; once they have trapped you into being like everyone else you will never see your cup of stars again; don't do it; and the little girl glanced at her, and smiled a little subtle, dimpling, wholly comprehending smile, and shook her head stubbornly at the glass. Brave girl, Eleanor thought; wise, brave girl.

"You're spoiling her," the father said. "She ought not to be allowed these whims."

"Just this once," the mother said. She put down the glass of milk and touched the little girl gently on the hand. "Eat your ice cream," she said.

When they left, the little girl waved good-by to Eleanor, and Eleanor waved back, sitting in joyful loneliness to finish her coffee while the gay stream tumbled along below her. I have not very much farther to go, Eleanor thought; I am more than halfway there. Journey's end, she thought, and far back in her mind, sparkling like the little stream, a tag end of a tune danced through her head, bringing distantly a word or so; "In delay there lies no plenty," she thought, "in delay there lies no plenty."

She nearly stopped forever just outside Ashton, because she came to a tiny cottage buried in a garden. I could live there all alone, she thought, slowing the car to look down the winding garden path to the small blue front door with, perfectly, a white cat on the step. No one would ever find me there, either, behind all those roses, and just to make sure I would plant oleanders by the road. I will light a fire in the cool evenings and toast apples at my own hearth. I will raise white cats and sew white curtains for the windows and sometimes come out of my door to go to the store to buy cinnamon and tea and thread. People will come to me to have their fortunes told, and I will brew love potions for sad maidens; I will have a robin. . . . But the cottage was far behind, and it was time to look for her new road, so carefully charted by Dr. Montague.

"Turn left onto Route 5 going west," his letter said, and, as efficiently and promptly as though he had been guiding her from some spot far away, moving her car with controls in his hands, it was done; she was on Route 5 going west, and her journey was nearly done. In spite of what he said, though, she thought, I will stop in Hillsdale for a minute, just for a cup of coffee, because I cannot bear to have my long trip end so soon. It was not really disobeying, anyway; the letter said it was inadvisable to stop in Hillsdale to ask the way, not forbidden to stop for coffee, and perhaps if I don't mention Hill House I will not be doing wrong. Anyway, she thought obscurely, it's my last chance.

Hillsdale was upon her before she knew it, a tangled, disorderly mess of dirty houses and crooked streets. It was small; once she had come onto the main street she could see the corner at the end with the gas station and the church. There seemed to be only one place to stop for coffee, and that was an unattractive diner, but Eleanor was bound to stop in Hillsdale and so she brought her car to the broken curb in front of the diner and got out. After a minute's thought, with a silent nod to Hillsdale, she locked the car, mindful of her suitcase on the floor and the carton on the back seat. I will not spend long in Hillsdale, she thought, looking up and down the street, which managed, even in the sunlight, to be dark and ugly. A dog slept uneasily in the shade against a wall, a woman stood in a doorway across the street and looked at Eleanor, and two young boys lounged against a fence, elaborately silent. Eleanor, who was afraid of strange dogs and jeering women and young hoodlums, went quickly into the diner, clutching her pocketbook and her car keys. Inside, she found a counter with a chinless, tired girl behind it, and a man sitting at the end eating. She wondered briefly how hungry he must have been to come in here at all, when she looked at the gray counter and the smeared glass bowl over a plate of doughnuts. "Coffee," she said to the girl behind the counter, and the girl turned wearily and tumbled down a cup from the piles on the shelves; I will have to drink this coffee because I said I was going to, Eleanor told herself sternly, but next time I will listen to Dr. Montague.

There was some elaborate joke going on between the man eating and the girl behind the counter; when she set Eleanor's coffee down she glanced at him and half-smiled, and he shrugged, and then the girl laughed. Eleanor looked up, but the girl was examining her fingernails and the man was wiping his plate with bread. Perhaps Eleanor's coffee was poisoned; it certainly looked it. Determined to plumb the village of Hillsdale to its lowest depths, Eleanor said to the girl, "I'll have one of those doughnuts too, please," and the girl, glancing sideways at the man, slid one of the doughnuts onto a dish and set it down in front of Eleanor and laughed when she caught another look from the man.

"This is a pretty little town," Eleanor said to the girl. "What is it called?"

The girl stared at her; perhaps no one had ever before had the audacity to call Hillsdale a pretty little town; after a moment the girl looked again at the man, as though calling for confirmation, and said, "Hillsdale."

"Have you lived here long?" Eleanor asked. I'm not going to mention Hill House, she assured Dr. Montague far away, I just want to waste a little time.

"Yeah," the girl said.

"It must be pleasant, living in a small town like this. I come from the city."

"Yeah?"

"Do you like it here?"

"It's all right," the girl said. She looked again at the man, who was listening carefully. "Not much to do."

"How large a town is it?"

"Pretty small. You want more coffee?" This was addressed to the man, who was rattling his cup against his saucer, and Eleanor took a first, shuddering sip of her own coffee and wondered how he could possibly want more.

"Do you have a lot of visitors around here?" she asked when the girl had filled the coffee cup and gone back to lounge against the shelves. "Tourists, I mean?"

"What for?" For a minute the girl flashed at her, from what might have been an emptiness greater than any Eleanor had ever known. "Why would anybody come *here?*" She looked sullenly at the man and added, "There's not even a movie."

"But the hills are so pretty. Mostly, with small out-of-the-way towns like this one, you'll find city people who have come and built themselves homes up in the hills. For privacy."

The girl laughed shortly. "Not *here* they don't."

"Or remodeling old houses—"

"Privacy," the girl said, and laughed again.

"It just seems surprising," Eleanor said, feeling the man looking at her.

"Yeah," the girl said. "If they'd put in a movie, even."

"I thought," Eleanor said carefully, "that I might even look around. Old houses are usually cheap, you know, and it's fun to make them over."

"Not around here," the girl said.

"Then," Eleanor said, "there are no old houses around here? Back in the hills?"

"Nope."

The man rose, taking change from his pocket, and spoke for the first time. "People *leave* this town," he said. "They don't *come* here."

When the door closed behind him the girl turned her flat eyes back to Eleanor, almost resentfully, as though Eleanor with her chatter had driven the man away. "He was right," she said finally. "They go away, the lucky ones."

"Why don't *you* run away?" Eleanor asked her, and the girl shrugged.

"Would I be any better off?" she asked. She took Eleanor's money without interest and returned the change. Then, with another of her quick flashes, she glanced at the empty plates at the end of the counter and almost smiled. "He comes in every day," she said. When Eleanor smiled back and started to speak, the girl turned her back and busied herself with the cups on the shelves, and Eleanor, feeling herself dismissed, rose gratefully from her coffee and took up her car keys and pocketbook. "Good-by," Eleanor said, and the girl, back still turned, said, "Good luck to you. I hope you find your house."

5

The road leading away from the gas station and the church was very poor indeed, deeply rutted and rocky. Eleanor's little car stumbled and bounced, reluctant to go farther into these unattractive hills, where the day seemed quickly drawing to an end under the thick, oppressive trees on either side. They do not really seem to have much traffic on this road, Eleanor thought wryly, turning the wheel quickly to avoid a particularly vicious rock ahead; six miles of this will not do the car any good; and for the first time in hours she thought of her sister and laughed. By now they would surely know that she had taken the car and gone, but they would not know where; they would be telling each other incredulously that they would never have suspected it of Eleanor. I would never have suspected it of myself, she thought, laughing still; everything is different, I am a new person, very far from home. "In delay there lies no plenty; . . . present mirth hath present laughter. . . ." And she gasped as the car cracked against a rock and reeled back across the road with an ominous scraping somewhere beneath, but then gathered itself together valiantly and resumed its dogged climb. The tree branches brushed against the windshield, and it grew steadily darker; Hill House likes to make an entrance, she thought; I wonder if the sun ever shines along here. At last, with one final effort, the car cleared a tangle of dead leaves and small branches across the road, and came into a clearing by the gate of Hill House.

Why am I here? she thought helplessly and at once; why am I here? The gate was tall and ominous and heavy, set strongly into a stone wall which went off through the trees. Even from the car she could see the padlock and the chain that was twisted around and through the bars. Beyond the gate she could see only that the road continued, turned, shadowed on either side by the still, dark trees.

Since the gate was so clearly locked—locked and double-locked and chained and barred; who, she wondered, wants so badly to get in?—she made no attempt to get out of her car, but pressed the horn, and the trees and the gate shuddered and withdrew slightly from the sound. After a minute she blew the horn again and then saw a man coming toward her from inside the gate; he was as dark and unwelcoming as the padlock, and before he moved toward the gate he peered through the bars at her, scowling.

"What *you* want?" His voice was sharp, mean.

"I want to come in, please. Please unlock the gate."

"Who say?"

"Why—" She faltered. "I'm supposed to come in," she said at last.

"What for?"

"I am expected." Or am I? she wondered suddenly; is this as far as I go?

"Who by?"

She knew, of course, that he was delighting in exceeding his authority, as though once he moved to unlock the gate he would lose the little temporary superiority he thought he had—and what superiority have I? she wondered; I am *outside* the gate, after all. She could already see that losing her temper, which she did rarely because she was so afraid of being ineffectual, would only turn him away, leaving her still outside the gate, railing futilely. She could even anticipate his innocence if he were reproved later for this arrogance—the maliciously vacant grin, the wide, blank eyes, the whining voice protesting that he *would* have let her in, he *planned* to let her in, but how could he be sure? He had his orders, didn't he? And he had to do what he was told? *He*'d be the one to get in trouble, wouldn't he, if he let in someone wasn't supposed to be inside? She could anticipate his shrug, and, picturing him, laughed, perhaps the worst thing she could have done.

Eying her, he moved back from the gate. "You better come back later," he said, and turned his back with an air of virtuous triumph.

"Listen," she called after him, still trying not to sound angry, "I am one of Doctor Montague's guests; he will be expecting me in the house—please *listen* to me!"

He turned and grinned at her. "They couldn't rightly be *expecting* you," he said, "seeing as you're the only one's *come*, so far."

"Do you mean that there's no one in the house?"

"No one *I* know of. Maybe my wife, getting it fixed up. So they couldn't be there exactly *expecting* you, now *could* they?"

She sat back against the car seat and closed her eyes. Hill House, she thought, you're as hard to get into as heaven.

"I suppose you know what you're *asking* for, coming here? I suppose they told you, back in the city? You *hear* anything about this place?"

"I heard that I was invited here as a guest of Doctor Montague's. When you open the gates I will go inside."

"I'll open them; I'm going to open them. I just want to be sure you know what's waiting for you in there. You ever been here before? One of the family, maybe?" He looked at her now, peering through the bars, his jeering face one more barrier, after padlock and chain. "I can't let you in till I'm *sure*, can I? What'd you say your name was?"

She sighed. "Eleanor Vance."

"Not one of the family then, I guess. You ever hear anything about this place?"

It's my chance, I suppose, she thought; I'm being given a last chance. I could turn my car around right here and now in front of these gates and go away from here, and no one would blame me. Anyone has a right to run away. She put her head out through the car window and said with fury, "My name is Eleanor Vance. I am expected in Hill House. Unlock those gates at once."

"All right, all *right*." Deliberately, making a wholly unnecessary display of fitting the key and turning it, he opened the padlock and loosened the chain and swung the gates just wide enough for the car to come through. Eleanor moved the car slowly, but the alacrity with which he leaped to the side of the road made her think for a minute that he had perceived the fleeting impulse crossing her mind; she laughed, and then stopped the car because he was coming toward her—safely, from the side.

"You won't like it," he said. "You'll be sorry I ever opened that gate."

"Out of the way, please," she said. "You've held me up long enough."

"You think they could get anyone else to open this gate? You think anyone else'd stay around here that long, except me and my wife? You think we can't have things just about the way we want them, long as we stay around here and fix up the house and open the gates for all you city people think you know everything?"

"Please get away from my car." She dared not admit to herself that he frightened her, for fear that he might perceive it; his nearness, leaning against the side of the car, was ugly, and his enormous resentment puzzled her; she had certainly made him open the gate for her, but did he think of the house and gardens inside as his own? A name from Dr. Montague's letter came into her mind, and she asked curiously, "Are you Dudley, the caretaker?"

"Yes, I'm Dudley, the caretaker." He mimicked her. "Who else you think would be around here?"

The honest old family retainer, she thought, proud and loyal and thoroughly unpleasant. "You and your wife take care of the house all alone?"

"Who else?" It was his boast, his curse, his refrain.

She moved restlessly, afraid to draw away from him too obviously, and yet wanting, with small motions of starting the car, to make him stand aside. "I'm sure you'll be able to make us very comfortable, you and your wife," she said, putting a tone of finality into her voice. "Meanwhile, I'm very anxious to get to the house as soon as possible."

He snickered disagreeably. "*Me*, now," he said, "me, I don't hang around here after dark."

Grinning, satisfied with himself, he stood away from the car, and Eleanor was grateful, although awkward starting the car under his eye; perhaps he will keep popping out at me all along the drive, she thought, a sneering Cheshire Cat, yelling each time that I should be happy to find anyone willing to hang around this place, until dark, anyway. To show that she was not at all affected by the thought of the face of Dudley the caretaker between the trees she began to whistle, a little annoyed to find that the same tune still ran through her head. "Present mirth hath present laughter . . ." And she told herself crossly that she must really make an effort to think of something else; she was sure that the rest of the words must be most unsuitable, to hide so stubbornly from her memory, and probably wholly disreputable to be caught singing on her arrival at Hill House.

Over the trees, occasionally, between them and the hills, she caught glimpses of what must be the roofs, perhaps a tower, of Hill House. They made houses so oddly back when Hill House was built, she thought; they put towers and turrets and buttresses and wooden lace on them, even sometimes Gothic spires and gargoyles; nothing was ever left undecorated. Perhaps Hill House has a tower, or a secret chamber, or even a passageway going off into the hills and probably used by smugglers—although what could smugglers find to smuggle around these lonely hills? Perhaps I will encounter a devilishly handsome smuggler and . . .

She turned her car onto the last stretch of straight drive

leading her directly, face to face, to Hill House and, moving without thought, pressed her foot on the brake to stall the car and sat, staring.

The house was vile. She shivered and thought, the words coming freely into her mind, Hill House is vile, it is diseased; get away from here at once.

2

~~~~~~

NO HUMAN eye can isolate the unhappy coincidence of line and place which suggests evil in the face of a house, and yet somehow a maniac juxtaposition, a badly turned angle, some chance meeting of roof and sky, turned Hill House into a place of despair, more frightening because the face of Hill House seemed awake, with a watchfulness from the blank windows and a touch of glee in the eyebrow of a cornice. Almost any house, caught unexpectedly or at an odd angle, can turn a deeply humorous look on a watching person; even a mischievous little chimney, or a dormer like a dimple, can catch up a beholder with a sense of fellowship; but a house arrogant and hating, never off guard, can only be evil. This house, which seemed somehow to have formed itself, flying together into its own powerful pattern under the hands of its builders, fitting itself into its own construction of lines and angles, reared its great head back against the sky without concession to humanity. It was a house without kindness, never meant to be lived in, not a fit place for people or for love or for hope. Exorcism cannot alter the countenance of a house; Hill House would stay as it was until it was destroyed.

I should have turned back at the gate, Eleanor thought. The house had caught her with an atavistic turn in the pit of the stomach, and she looked along the lines of its roofs, fruitlessly endeavoring to locate the badness, whatever dwelt there; her hands turned nervously cold so that she fumbled, trying to take out a cigarette, and beyond everything else she was afraid, listening to the sick voice inside her which whispered, *Get away from here, get away.*

But this is what I came so far to find, she told herself; I can't go back. Besides, he would laugh at me if I tried to get back out through that gate.

Trying not to look up at the house—and she could not even have told its color, or its style, or its size, except that it was enormous and dark, looking down over her—she started the car again, and drove up the last bit of driveway directly to the steps, which led in a forthright, no-escape manner onto the veranda and aimed at the front door. The drive turned off on either side, to encircle the house, and probably later she could take her car around and find a building of some kind to put it in; now she felt uneasily that she did not care to cut off her means of departure too completely. She turned the car just enough to move it off to one side, out of the way of later arrivals—it would be a pity, she thought grimly, for anyone to get a first look at this house with anything so comforting as a human automobile parked in front of it—and got out, taking her suitcase and her coat. Well, she thought inadequately, here I am.

It was an act of moral strength to lift her foot and set it on the bottom step, and she thought that her deep unwillingness to touch Hill House for the first time came directly from the vivid feeling that it was waiting for her, evil, but patient. Journeys end in lovers meeting, she thought, remembering her song at last, and laughed, standing on the steps of Hill House, journeys end in lovers meeting, and she put her feet down firmly and went up to the veranda and the door. Hill House came around her in a rush; she was enshadowed, and the sound of her feet on the wood of the veranda was an outrage in the utter silence, as though it had been a very long time since feet stamped across the boards of Hill House. She brought her hand up to the heavy iron knocker that had a child's face, determined to make more noise and yet more, so that Hill House might be very sure she was there, and then the door opened without warning and she was looking at a woman who, if like ever merited like, could only be the wife of the man at the gate.

"Mrs. Dudley?" she said, catching her breath. "I'm Eleanor Vance. I'm expected."

Silently the woman stood aside. Her apron was clean, her hair was neat, and yet she gave an indefinable air of dirtiness, quite in keeping with her husband, and the suspicious sullenness of her face was a match for the malicious petulance of his. No, Eleanor told herself; it's partly because everything seems so dark around here, and partly because I expected that man's wife to be ugly. If I hadn't seen Hill House, would I be so unfair to these people? They only take care of it, after all.

The hall in which they stood was overfull of dark wood and weighty carving, dim under the heaviness of the staircase, which lay back from the farther end. Above there seemed to be another hallway, going the width of the house; she could see a wide landing and then, across the staircase well, doors closed along the upper hall. On either side of her now were great double doors, carved with fruit and grain and living things; all the doors she could see in this house were closed.

When she tried to speak, her voice was drowned in the dim stillness, and she had to try again to make a sound. "Can you take me to my room?" she asked at last, gesturing toward her suitcase on the floor and watching the wavering reflection of her hand going down and down into the deep shadows of the polished floor, "I gather I'm the first one here. You—you *did* say you were Mrs. Dudley?" I think I'm going to cry, she thought, like a child sobbing and wailing, *I don't like it here.* . . .

Mrs. Dudley turned and started up the stairs, and Eleanor took up her suitcase and followed, hurrying after anything else alive in this house. No, she thought, I don't like it here. Mrs. Dudley came to the top of the stairs and turned right, and Eleanor saw that with some rare perception the builders of the house had given up any attempt at style—probably after realizing what the house was going to be, whether they chose it or not—and had, on this second floor, set in a long, straight hall to accommodate the doors to the bedrooms; she had a quick impression of the builders finishing off the second and third stories of the house with a kind of indecent haste, eager to finish their work without embellishment and get out of there, following the simplest possible pattern for the rooms. At the left end of the hall was a second staircase, probably going from servants' rooms on the third floor down past the second to the service rooms below; at the right end of the hall another room had been set in, perhaps, since it was on the end, to get the maximum amount of sun and light. Except for a continuation of the dark woodwork, and what looked like a series of poorly executed engravings arranged with unlovely exactness along the hall in either direction, nothing broke the straightness of the hall except the series of doors, all closed.

Mrs. Dudley crossed the hall and opened a door, perhaps at random. "This is the blue room," she said.

From the turn in the staircase Eleanor assumed that the room would be at the front of the house; sister Anne, sister Anne, she thought, and moved gratefully toward the light from the room. "How nice," she said, standing in the doorway, but only from the sense that she must say something; it was not nice at all, and only barely tolerable; it held enclosed the same clashing disharmony that marked Hill House throughout.

Mrs. Dudley turned aside to let Eleanor come in, and spoke, apparently to the wall. "I set dinner on the dining-room sideboard at six sharp," she said. "You can serve yourselves. I clear up in the morning. I have breakfast ready for you at nine. That's the way I agreed to do. I can't keep the rooms up the way you'd like, but there's no one else you could get that would help me. I don't wait on people. What I agreed to, it doesn't mean I wait on people."

Eleanor nodded, standing uncertainly in the doorway.

"I don't stay after I set out dinner," Mrs. Dudley went on. "Not after it begins to get dark. I leave before dark comes."

"I know," Eleanor said.

"We live over in the town, six miles away."

"Yes," Eleanor said, remembering Hillsdale.

"So there won't be anyone around if you need help."

"I understand."

"We couldn't even hear you, in the night."

"I don't suppose—"

"No one could. No one lives any nearer than the town. No one else will come any nearer than that."

"I know," Eleanor said tiredly.

"In the night," Mrs. Dudley said, and smiled outright. "In the dark," she said, and closed the door behind her.

Eleanor almost giggled, thinking of herself calling, "Oh, Mrs. Dudley, I need your help in the dark," and then she shivered.

2

She stood alone beside her suitcase, her coat still hanging over her arm, thoroughly miserable, telling herself helplessly, Journeys end in lovers meeting, and wishing she could go home. Behind her lay the dark staircase and the polished hallway and the great front door and Mrs. Dudley and Dudley laughing at the gate and the padlocks and Hillsdale and the cottage of flowers and the family at the inn and the oleander garden and the house with the stone lions in front, and they had brought her, under Dr. Montague's unerring eye, to the blue room at Hill House. It's awful, she thought, unwilling to move, since motion might imply acceptance, a gesture of moving in, it's awful and I don't want to stay; but there was nowhere else to go; Dr. Montague's letter had brought her this far and could take her no farther. After a minute she sighed and shook her head and walked across to set her suitcase down on the bed.

Here I am in the blue room of Hill House, she said half aloud, although it was real enough, and beyond all question a blue room. There were blue dimity curtains over the two windows, which looked out over the roof of the veranda onto the lawn, and a blue figured rug on the floor, and a blue spread on the bed and a blue quilt at the foot. The walls, dark woodwork to shoulder height, were blue-figured paper above, with a design of tiny blue flowers, wreathed and gathered and delicate. Perhaps someone had once hoped to lighten the air of the blue room in Hill House with a dainty wallpaper, not seeing how such a hope would evaporate in Hill House, leaving only the faintest hint of its existence, like an almost inaudible echo of sobbing far away. . . . Eleanor shook herself, turning to see the room complete. It had an unbelievably faulty design which left it chillingly wrong in all its dimensions, so that the walls seemed always in one direction a fraction longer than the eye could endure, and in another direction a fraction less than the barest possible tolerable length; this is where they want me to *sleep*, Eleanor thought incredulously; what nightmares are waiting, shadowed, in those high corners— what breath of mindless fear will drift across my mouth

. . . and shook herself again. *Really*, she told herself, *really*, Eleanor.

She opened her suitcase on the high bed and, slipping off her stiff city shoes with grateful relief, began to unpack, at the back of her mind the thoroughly female conviction that the best way to soothe a troubled mind is to put on comfortable shoes. Yesterday, packing her suitcase in the city, she had chosen clothes which she assumed would be suitable for wearing in an isolated country house; she had even run out at the last minute and bought—excited at her own daring—two pairs of slacks, something she had not worn in more years than she could remember. Mother would be *furious*, she had thought, packing the slacks down at the bottom of her suitcase so that she need not take them out, need never let anyone know she had them, in case she lost her courage. Now, in Hill House, they no longer seemed so new; she unpacked carelessly, setting dresses crookedly on hangers, tossing the slacks into the bottom drawer of the high marble-topped dresser, throwing her city shoes into a corner of the great wardrobe. She was bored already with the books she had brought; I am probably not going to stay anyway, she thought, and closed her empty suitcase and set it in the wardrobe corner; it won't take me five minutes to pack again. She discovered that she had been trying to put her suitcase down without making a sound and then realized that while she unpacked she had been in her stocking feet, trying to move as silently as possible, as though stillness were vital in Hill House; she remembered that Mrs. Dudley had also walked without sound. When she stood still in the middle of the room the pressing silence of Hill House came back all around her.

I am like a small creature swallowed whole by a monster, she thought, and the monster feels my tiny little movements inside. "No," she said aloud, and the one word echoed. She went quickly across the room and pushed aside the blue dimity curtains, but the sunlight came only palely through the thick glass of the windows, and she could see only the roof of the veranda and a stretch of the lawn beyond. Somewhere down there was her little car, which could take her away again. Journeys end in lovers meeting, she thought; it was my own choice to come. Then she realized that she was afraid to go back across the room.

She was standing with her back to the window, looking from the door to the wardrobe to the dresser to the bed, telling herself that she was not afraid at all, when she heard, far below, the sounds of a car door slamming and then quick footsteps, almost dancing, up the steps and across the veranda, and then, shockingly, the crash of the great iron knocker coming down. Why, she thought, there are other people coming; I am not going to be here all alone. Almost laughing, she ran across the room and into the hall, to look down the staircase into the hallway below.

"Thank heaven you're here," she said, peering through the dimness, "thank heaven somebody's here." She realized without surprise that she was speaking as though Mrs. Dudley could not hear her, although Mrs. Dudley stood, straight and pale, in the hall. "Come on up," Eleanor said, "you'll have to carry your own suitcase." She was breathless and seemed unable to stop talking, her usual shyness melted away by relief. "My name's Eleanor Vance," she said, "and I'm so glad you're here."

"I'm Theodora. Just Theodora. This *bloody* house—"

"It's just as bad up here. Come on up. Make her give you the room next to mine."

Theodora came up the heavy stairway after Mrs. Dudley, looking incredulously at the stained-glass window on the landing, the marble urn in a niche, the patterned carpet. Her suitcase was considerably larger than Eleanor's, and considerably more luxurious, and Eleanor came forward to help her, glad that her own things were safely put away out of sight. "Wait till you see the bedrooms," Eleanor said. "Mine used to be the embalming room, I think."

"It's the home I've always dreamed of," Theodora said. "A little hideaway where I can be alone with my thoughts. Particularly if my thoughts happened to be about murder or suicide or—"

"Green room," Mrs. Dudley said coldly, and Eleanor sensed, with a quick turn of apprehension, that flippant or critical talk about the house bothered Mrs. Dudley in some manner; maybe she thinks it can hear us, Eleanor thought, and then was sorry she had thought it. Perhaps she shivered, because Theodora turned with a quick smile and touched her shoulder gently, reassuringly; she is charming, Eleanor thought, smiling back, not at all the sort of person who belongs in this dreary, dark place, but then, probably, I don't belong here either; I am not the sort of person for Hill House but I can't think of anybody who would be. She laughed then, watching Theodora's expression as she stood in the doorway of the green room.

"Good Lord," Theodora said, looking sideways at Eleanor. "How perfectly enchanting. A positive bower."

"I set dinner on the dining-room sideboard at six sharp," Mrs. Dudley said. "You can serve yourselves. I clear up in the morning. I have breakfast ready for you at nine. That's the way I agreed to do."

"You're frightened," Theodora said, watching Eleanor.

"I can't keep the rooms up the way you'd like, but there's no one else you could get that would help me. I don't wait on people. What I agreed to, it doesn't mean I wait on people."

"It was just when I thought I was all alone," Eleanor said.

"I don't stay after six. Not after it begins to get dark."

"I'm here now," Theodora said, "so it's all right."

"We have a connecting bathroom," Eleanor said absurdly. "The rooms are exactly alike."

Green dimity curtains hung over the windows in Theodora's room, the wallpaper was decked with green garlands, the bedspread and quilt were green, the marble-topped dresser and the huge wardrobe were the same. "I've never seen such awful places in my *life*," Eleanor said, her voice rising.

"Like the very best hotels," Theodora said, "or any good girl's camp."

"I leave before dark comes," Mrs. Dudley went on.

"No one can hear you if you scream in the night," Eleanor told Theodora. She realized that she was clutching at the doorknob and, under Theodora's quizzical eye, unclenched her fingers and walked steadily across the room. "We'll have to find some way of opening these windows," she said.

"So there won't be anyone around if you need help," Mrs. Dudley said. "We couldn't hear you, even in the night. No one could."

"All right now?" Theodora asked, and Eleanor nodded. "No one lives any nearer than the town. No one else will come any nearer than that."

"You're probably just hungry," Theodora said. "And I'm starved myself." She set her suitcase on the bed and slipped off her shoes. "*Nothing*," she said, "upsets me more than being hungry; I snarl and snap and burst into tears." She lifted a pair of softly tailored slacks out of the suitcase.

"In the night," Mrs. Dudley said. She smiled. "In the dark," she said, and closed the door behind her.

After a minute Eleanor said, "She also walks without making a sound."

"Delightful old body." Theodora turned, regarding her room. "I take it back, that about the best hotels," she said. "It's a little bit like a boarding school I went to for a while."

"Come and see mine," Eleanor said. She opened the bathroom door and led the way into her blue room. "I was all unpacked and thinking about packing again when you came."

"Poor baby. You're certainly starving. All *I* could think of when I got a look at the place from outside was what fun it would be to stand out there and watch it burn down. Maybe before we leave . . ."

"It was terrible, being here alone."

"You should have seen that boarding school of mine during vacations." Theodora went back into her own room and, with the sense of movement and sound in the two rooms, Eleanor felt more cheerful. She straightened her clothes on the hangers in the wardrobe and set her books evenly on the bed table. "You know," Theodora called from the other room, "it *is* kind of like the first day at school; everything's ugly and strange, and you don't know anybody, and you're afraid everyone's going to laugh at your clothes."

Eleanor, who had opened the dresser drawer to take out a pair of slacks, stopped and then laughed and threw the slacks on the bed.

"Did I understand correctly," Theodora went on, "that Mrs. Dudley is not going to come if we scream in the night?"

"It was not what she agreed to. Did you meet the amiable old retainer at the gate?"

"We had a lovely chat. He said I couldn't come in and I said I could and then I tried to run him down with my car but he jumped. Look, do you think we have to sit around here in our rooms and wait? I'd like to change into something comfortable—unless we dress for dinner, do you think?"

"I won't if you won't."

"I won't if *you* won't. They can't fight both of us. Anyway, let's get out of here and go exploring; I would very much like to get this roof off from over my head."

"It gets dark so early, in these hills, with all the trees . . ." Eleanor went to the window again, but there was still sunlight slanting across the lawn.

"It won't be really dark for nearly an hour. I want to go outside and roll on the grass."

Eleanor chose a red sweater, thinking that in this room in this house the red of the sweater and the red of the sandals bought to match it would almost certainly be utterly at war with each other, although they had been close enough yesterday in the city. Serves me right anyway, she thought, for wanting to wear such things; I never did before. But she looked oddly well, it seemed to her as she stood by the long mirror on the wardrobe door, almost comfortable. "Do you have any idea who else is coming?" she asked. "Or when?"

"Doctor Montague," Theodora said. "I thought he'd be here before anyone else."

"Have you known Doctor Montague long?"

"Never met him," Theodora said. "Have you?"

"Never. You almost ready?"

"All ready." Theodora came through the bathroom door into Eleanor's room; she is lovely, Eleanor thought, turning to look; I wish I were lovely. Theodora was wearing a vivid yellow shirt, and Eleanor laughed and said, "You bring more light into this room than the window."

Theodora came over and regarded herself approvingly in Eleanor's mirror. "I feel," she said, "that in this dreary place it is our duty to look as bright as possible. I approve of your red sweater; the two of us will be visible from one end of Hill House to the other." Still looking into the mirror, she asked, "I suppose Doctor Montague wrote to you?"

"Yes." Eleanor was embarrassed. "I didn't know, at first, whether it was a joke or not. But my brother-in-law checked up on him."

"You know," Theodora said slowly, "up until the last minute—when I got to the gates, I guess—I never really thought there *would* be a Hill House. You don't go around expecting things like this to happen."

"But some of us go around hoping," Eleanor said.

Theodora laughed and swung around before the mirror and caught Eleanor's hand. "Fellow babe in the woods," she said, "let's go exploring."

"We can't go far away from the house—"

"I promise not to go one step farther than you say. Do you think we have to check in and out with Mrs. Dudley?"

"She probably watches every move we make, anyway; it's probably part of what she agreed to."

"Agreed to with whom, I wonder? Count Dracula?"

"You think *he* lives in Hill House?"

"I think he spends all his week ends here; I swear I saw bats in the woodwork downstairs. Follow, follow."

They ran downstairs, moving with color and life against the dark woodwork and the clouded light of the stairs, their feet clattering, and Mrs. Dudley stood below and watched them in silence.

"We're going exploring, Mrs. Dudley," Theodora said lightly. "We'll be outside somewhere."

"But we'll be back soon," Eleanor added.

"I set dinner on the sideboard at six o'clock," Mrs. Dudley explained.

Eleanor, tugging, got the great front door open; it was just as heavy as it looked, and she thought, We will really have to find some easier way to get back in. "Leave this open," she said over her shoulder to Theodora. "It's terribly heavy. Get one of those big vases and prop it open."

Theodora wheeled one of the big stone vases from the corner of the hall, and they stood it in the doorway and rested the door against it. The fading sunlight outside was bright after the darkness of the house, and the air was fresh and sweet. Behind them Mrs. Dudley moved the vase again, and the big door slammed shut.

"Lovable old thing," Theodora said to the closed door. For a moment her face was thin with anger, and Eleanor thought, I hope she never looks at *me* like that, and was surprised, remembering that she was always shy with strangers, awkward and timid, and yet had come in no more than half an hour to think of Theodora as close and vital, someone whose anger would be frightening. "I think," Eleanor said hesitantly, and relaxed, because when she spoke Theodora turned and smiled again, "I think that during the daylight hours when Mrs. Dudley is around I shall find myself some absorbing occupation far, far from the house. Rolling the tennis court, perhaps. Or tending the grapes in the hothouse."

"Perhaps you could help Dudley with the gates."

"Or look for nameless graves in the nettlepatch."

They were standing by the rail of the veranda; from there they could see down the drive to the point where it turned among the trees again, and down over the soft curve of the hills to the distant small line which might have been the main highway, the road back to the cities from which they had come. Except for the wires which ran to the house from a spot among the trees, there was no evidence that Hill House belonged in any way to the rest of the world. Eleanor turned and followed the veranda; it went, apparently, all around the house. "Oh, look," she said, turning the corner.

Behind the house the hills were piled in great pressing masses, flooded with summer green now, rich, and still.

"It's why they called it Hill House," Eleanor said inadequately.

"It's altogether Victorian," Theodora said. "They simply wallowed in this kind of great billowing overdone sort of thing and buried themselves in folds of velvet and tassels and purple plush. Anyone before them or after would have put this house right up there on *top* of those hills where it belongs, instead of snuggling it down here."

"If it were on top of the hill everyone could see it. I vote for keeping it well hidden where it is."

"All the time I'm here I'm going to be terrified," Theodora said, "thinking one of those hills will fall on us."

"They don't fall on you. They just slide down, silently and secretly, rolling over you while you try to run away."

"Thank you," Theodora said in a small voice. "What Mrs. Dudley has started you have completed nicely. I shall pack and go home at once."

Believing her for a minute, Eleanor turned and stared, and then saw the amusement on her face and thought, She's much braver than I am. Unexpectedly—although it was later to become a familiar note, a recognizable attribute of what was to mean "Theodora" in Eleanor's mind—Theodora caught at Eleanor's thought, and answered her. "Don't be so afraid all the time," she said and reached out to touch Eleanor's cheek with one finger. "We never know where our courage is coming from." Then, quickly, she ran down the steps and out onto the lawn between the tall grouped trees. "Hurry," she called back, "I want to see if there's a brook somewhere."

"We can't go too far," Eleanor said, following. Like two

children they ran across the grass, both welcoming the sudden openness of clear spaces after even a little time in Hill House, their feet grateful for the grass after the solid floors; with an instinct almost animal, they followed the sound and smell of water. "Over here," Theodora said, "a little path."

It led them tantalizingly closer to the sound of the water, doubling back and forth through the trees, giving them occasional glimpses down the hill to the driveway, leading them around out of sight of the house across a rocky meadow, and always downhill. As they came away from the house and out of the trees to places where the sunlight could still find them Eleanor was easier, although she could see that the sun was dropping disturbingly closer to the heaped hills. She called to Theodora, but Theodora only called back, "Follow, follow," and ran down the path. Suddenly she stopped, breathless and tottering, on the very edge of the brook, which had leaped up before her almost without warning; Eleanor, coming more slowly behind, caught at her hand and held her back and then, laughing, they fell together against the bank which sloped sharply down to the brook.

"They like to surprise you around here," Theodora said, gasping.

"Serve you right if you went diving in," Eleanor said. "Running like that."

"It's pretty, isn't it?" The water of the brook moved quickly in little lighted ripples; on the other side the grass grew down to the edge of the water and yellow and blue flowers leaned their heads over; there was a rounded soft hill there, and perhaps more meadow beyond, and, far away, the great hills, still catching the light of the sun. "It's pretty," Theodora said with finality.

"I'm sure I've been here before," Eleanor said. "In a book of fairy tales, perhaps."

"I'm sure of it. Can you skip rocks?"

"This is where the princess comes to meet the magic golden fish who is really a prince in disguise—"

"He couldn't draw much water, that golden fish of yours; it can't be more than three inches deep."

"There are stepping stones to go across, and *little* fish swimming, tiny ones—minnows?"

"Princes in disguise, all of them." Theodora stretched in the sun on the bank, and yawned. "Tadpoles?" she suggested.

"Minnows. It's too late for tadpoles, silly, but I bet we can find frogs' eggs. I used to catch minnows in my hands and let them go."

"What a farmer's wife you might have made."

"This is a place for picnics, with lunch beside the brook and hard-boiled eggs."

Theodora laughed. "Chicken salad and chocolate cake."

"Lemonade in a Thermos bottle. Spilled salt."

Theodora rolled over luxuriously. "They're wrong about ants, you know. There were almost never ants. Cows, maybe, but I don't think I ever *did* see an ant on a picnic."

"Was there always a bull in a field? Did someone always say, 'But we can't go through that field; that's where the bull is'?"

Theodora opened one eye. "Did you use to have a comic uncle? Everyone always laughed, whatever he said? And he used to tell you not to be afraid of the bull—if the bull came after you all you had to do was grab the ring through his nose and swing him around your head?"

Eleanor tossed a pebble into the brook and watched it sink clearly to the bottom. "Did you have a lot of uncles?"

"Thousands. Do you?"

After a minute Eleanor said, "Oh, yes. Big ones and little ones and fat ones and thin ones—"

"Do you have an Aunt Edna?"

"Aunt Muriel."

"Kind of thin? Rimless glasses?"

"A garnet brooch," Eleanor said.

"Does she wear a kind of dark red dress to family parties?"

"Lace cuffs—"

"Then I think we must really be related," Theodora said. "Did you use to have braces on your teeth?"

"No. Freckles."

"I went to that private school where they made me learn to curtsy."

"I always had colds all winter long. My mother made me wear woollen stockings."

"*My* mother made my brother take me to dances, and I used to curtsy like mad. My brother still hates me."

"I fell down during the graduation procession."

"I forgot my lines in the operetta."

"I used to write poetry."

"Yes," Theodora said, "I'm positive we're cousins."

She sat up, laughing, and then Eleanor said, "Be quiet; there's something moving over there." Frozen, shoulders pressed together, they stared, watching the spot of hillside across the brook where the grass moved, watching something unseen move slowly across the bright green hill, chilling the sunlight and the dancing little brook. "What is it?" Eleanor said in a breath, and Theodora put a strong hand on her wrist.

"It's gone," Theodora said clearly, and the sun came back and it was warm again. "It was a rabbit," Theodora said.

"I couldn't see it," Eleanor said.

"I saw it the minute you spoke," Theodora said firmly. "It was a rabbit; it went over the hill and out of sight."

"We've been away too long," Eleanor said and looked up anxiously at the sun touching the hilltops. She got up quickly and found that her legs were stiff from kneeling on the damp grass.

"Imagine two splendid old picnic-going girls like us," Theodora said, "afraid of a rabbit."

Eleanor leaned down and held out a hand to help her up. "We'd really better hurry back," she said and, because she did not herself understand her compelling anxiety, added, "The others might be there by now."

"We'll have to come back here for a picnic soon," Theodora said, following carefully up the path, which went steadily uphill. "We really must have a good old-fashioned picnic down by the brook."

"We can ask Mrs. Dudley to hard-boil some eggs." Eleanor stopped on the path, not turning. "Theodora," she said,

"I don't think I can, you know. I don't think I really will be able to do it."

"Eleanor." Theodora put an arm across her shoulders. "Would you let them separate us now? Now that we've found out we're cousins?"

3

~~~~~~

THE SUN went down smoothly behind the hills, slipping almost eagerly, at last, into the pillowy masses. There
were already long shadows on the lawn as Eleanor and
Theodora came up the path toward the side veranda of
Hill House, blessedly hiding its mad face in the growing
darkness.

"There's someone waiting there," Eleanor said, walking
more quickly, and so saw Luke for the first time. Journeys
end in lovers meeting, she thought, and could only say inadequately, "Are you looking for us?"

He had come to the veranda rail, looking down at them in the dusk, and now he bowed with a deep welcoming gesture, " 'These being dead,' " he said, " 'then dead must I be.' Ladies, if you are the ghostly inhabitants of Hill House, I am here forever."

He's really kind of silly, Eleanor thought sternly, and Theodora said, "Sorry we weren't here to meet you; we've been exploring."

"A sour old beldame with a face of curds welcomed us, thank you," he said. " 'Howdy-do,' she told me, 'I hope I see you alive when I come back in the morning and your dinner's on the sideboard.' Saying which, she departed in a late-model convertible with First and Second Murderers."

"Mrs. Dudley," Theodora said. "First Murderer must be Dudley-at-the-gate; I suppose the other was Count Dracula. A wholesome family."

"Since we are listing our cast of characters," he said, "my name is Luke Sanderson."

Eleanor was startled into speaking. "Then you're one of the family? The people who own Hill House? Not one of Doctor Montague's guests?"

"I am one of the family; someday this stately pile will belong to me; until then, however, I am here as one of Doctor Montague's guests."

Theodora giggled. "*We*," she said, "are Eleanor and Theodora, two little girls who were planning a picnic down by the brook and got scared home by a rabbit."

"I go in mortal terror of rabbits," Luke agreed politely. "May I come if I carry the picnic basket?"

"You may bring your ukulele and strum to us while we eat chicken sandwiches. Is Doctor Montague here?"

"He's inside," Luke said, "gloating over his haunted house."

They were silent for a minute, wanting to move closer together, and then Theodora said thinly, "It doesn't sound so funny, does it, now it's getting dark?"

"Ladies, welcome." And the great front door opened. "Come inside. I am Doctor Montague."

2

The four of them stood, for the first time, in the wide, dark entrance hall of Hill House. Around them the house steadied and located them, above them the hills slept watchfully, small eddies of air and sound and movement stirred and waited and whispered, and the center of consciousness was somehow the small space where they stood, four separated people, and looked trustingly at one another.

"I am very happy that everyone arrived safely, and on time," Doctor Montague said. "Welcome, all of you, welcome to Hill House—although perhaps that sentiment ought to come more properly from you, my boy? In any case, welcome, welcome. Luke, my boy, can you make a martini?"

3

Dr. Montague raised his glass and sipped hopefully, and sighed. "Fair," he said. "Only fair, my boy. To our success at Hill House, however."

"How would one reckon success, exactly, in an affair like this?" Luke inquired curiously.

The doctor laughed. "Put it, then," he said, "that I hope that all of us will have an exciting visit and my book will rock my colleagues back on their heels. I cannot call your visit a vacation, although to some it might seem so, because I am hopeful of your working—although work, of course, depends largely upon what is to be done, does it not? Notes," he said with relief, as though fixing upon one unshakable solidity in a world of fog, "notes. We will take notes—to some, a not unbearable task."

"So long as no one makes any puns about spirits and spirits," Theodora said, holding out her glass to Luke to be filled.

"Spirits?" The doctor peered at her. "Spirits? Yes, indeed. Of course, none of *us* . . ." He hesitated, frowning. "Certainly not," he said and took three quick agitated sips at his cocktail.

"Everything's so strange," Eleanor said. "I mean, this morning I was wondering what Hill House would be like, and now I can't believe that it's real, and we're here."

They were sitting in a small room, chosen by the doctor, who had led them into it, down a narrow corridor, fumbling a little at first, but then finding his way. It was not a cozy room, certainly. It had an unpleasantly high ceiling, and a narrow tiled fireplace which looked chill in spite of the fire which Luke had lighted at once; the chairs in which they sat were rounded and slippery, and the light coming through the colored beaded shades of the lamps sent shadows into the corners. The overwhelming sense of the room was purple; beneath their feet the carpeting glowed in dim convoluted patterns, the walls were papered and gilt, and a marble cupid beamed fatuously down at them from the mantel. When they were silent for a moment the quiet weight of the house pressed down from all around them.

Eleanor, wondering if she were really here at all, and not dreaming of Hill House from some safe spot impossibly remote, looked slowly and carefully around the room, telling herself that this was real, these things existed, from the tiles around the fireplace to the marble cupid; these people were going to be her friends. The doctor was round and rosy and bearded and looked as though he might be more suitably established before a fire in a pleasant little sitting room, with a cat on his knee and a rosy little wife to bring him jellied scones, and yet he was undeniably the Dr. Montague who had guided Eleanor here, a little man both knowledgeable and stubborn. Across the fire from the doctor was Theodora, who had gone unerringly to the most nearly comfortable chair, had wriggled herself into it somehow with her legs over the arm and her head tucked in against the back; she was like a cat, Eleanor thought, and clearly a cat waiting for its dinner. Luke was not still for a minute, but moved back and forth across the shadows, filling glasses, stirring the fire, touching the marble cupid; he was bright in the firelight, and restless. They were all silent, looking into the fire, lazy after their several journeys, and Eleanor thought, I am the fourth person in this room; I am one of them; I belong.

"Since we *are* all here," Luke said suddenly, as though there had been no pause in the conversation, "shouldn't we get acquainted? We know only names, so far. I know that it is Eleanor, here, who is wearing a red sweater, and consequently it must be Theodora who wears yellow—"

"Doctor Montague has a beard," Theodora said, "so you must be Luke."

"And you are Theodora," Eleanor said, "because *I* am Eleanor." An Eleanor, she told herself triumphantly, who belongs, who is talking easily, who is sitting by the fire with her friends.

"Therefore *you* are wearing the red sweater," Theodora explained to her soberly.

"I have no beard," Luke said, "so *he* must be Doctor Montague."

"*I* have a beard," Dr. Montague said, pleased, and looked around at them with a happy beam. "My wife," he told them, "*likes* a man to wear a beard. Many women, on the other hand, find a beard distasteful. A clean-shaven man —you'll excuse me, my boy—never looks fully dressed, my wife tells me." He held out his glass to Luke.

"Now that I know which of us is me," Luke said, "let me identify myself further. I am, in private life—assuming that this is public life and the rest of the world *is* actually private—let me see, a bullfighter. Yes. A bullfighter."

"I love my love with a B," Eleanor said in spite of herself, "because he is bearded."

"Very true." Luke nodded at her. "That makes me Doctor Montague. I live in Bangkok, and my hobby is bothering women."

"Not at all," Dr. Montague protested, amused. "I live in Belmont."

Theodora laughed and gave Luke that quick, understanding glance she had earlier given Eleanor. Eleanor, watching, thought wryly that it might sometimes be oppressive to be for long around one so immediately in tune, so perceptive, as Theodora. "I am by profession an artist's model," Eleanor said quickly, to silence her own thoughts. "I live a mad, abandoned life, draped in a shawl and going from garret to garret."

"Are you heartless and wanton?" Luke asked. "Or are you one of the fragile creatures who will fall in love with a lord's son and pine away?"

"Losing all your beauty and coughing a good deal?" Theodora added.

"I rather think I have a heart of gold," Eleanor said reflectively. "At any rate, my affairs are the talk of the cafés." Dear me, she thought. Dear me.

"Alas," Theodora said, "I am a lord's *daughter*. Ordinarily I go clad in silk and lace and cloth of gold, but I have borrowed my maid's finery to appear among you. I may of course become so enamored of the common life that I will never go back, and the poor girl will have to get herself new clothes. And you, Doctor Montague?"

He smiled in the firelight. "A pilgrim. A wanderer."

"Truly a congenial little group," Luke said approvingly. "Destined to be inseparable friends, in fact. A courtesan, a pilgrim, a princess, and a bullfighter. Hill House has surely never seen our like."

"I will give the honor to Hill House," Theodora said. "I have never seen *its* like." She rose, carrying her glass, and went to examine a bowl of glass flowers. "What did they *call* this room, do you suppose?"

"A parlor, perhaps," Dr. Montague said. "Perhaps a boudoir. I thought we would be more comfortable in here than in one of the other rooms. As a matter of fact, I think we ought to regard this room as our center of operations, a kind of common room; it may not be cheerful—"

"Of *course* it's cheerful," Theodora said stanchly. "There is nothing more exhilarating than maroon upholstery and oak paneling, and what is that in the corner there? A sedan chair?"

"Tomorrow you will see the *other* rooms," the doctor told her.

"If we are going to have this for a rumpus room," Luke said, "I propose we move in something to sit on. I cannot perch for long on anything here; I skid," he said confidentially to Eleanor.

"Tomorrow," the doctor said. "Tomorrow, as a matter of fact, we will explore the entire house and arrange things to please ourselves. And now, if you have all finished, I suggest that we determine what Mrs. Dudley has done about our dinner."

Theodora moved at once and then stopped, bewildered. "Someone is going to have to lead me," she said. "I can't possibly tell where the dining room is." She pointed. "*That* door leads to the long passage and then into the front hall," she said.

The doctor chuckled. "Wrong, my dear. That door leads to the conservatory." He rose to lead the way. "*I* have studied a map of the house," he said complacently, "and I believe that we have only to go through the door here, down the passage, into the front hall, and across the hall and through the billiard room to find the dining room. Not hard," he said, "once you get into practice."

"Why did they mix themselves up so?" Theodora asked. "Why so many little odd rooms?"

"Maybe they liked to hide from each other," Luke said.

"*I* can't understand why they wanted everything so dark," Theodora said. She and Eleanor were following Dr. Montague down the passage, and Luke came behind, lingering to look into the drawer of a narrow table, and wondering aloud to himself at the valance of cupid-heads and ribbon-bunches which topped the paneling in the dark hall.

"Some of these rooms are entirely inside rooms," the doctor said from ahead of them. "No windows, no access to the outdoors at all. However, a series of enclosed rooms is not altogether surprising in a house of this period, particularly when you recall that what windows they *did* have were heavily shrouded with hangings and draperies within, and shrubbery without. Ah." He opened the passage door and led them into the front hall. "Now," he said, considering the doorways opposite, two smaller doors flanking the great central double door; "Now," he said, and selected the nearest. "The house *does* have its little oddities," he continued, holding the door so that they might pass through into the dark room beyond. "Luke, come and hold this open so I can find the dining room." Moving cautiously, he crossed the dark room and opened a door, and they followed him into the pleasantest room they had seen so far, more pleasant, certainly, because of the lights and the sight and smell of food. "I congratulate myself," he said, rubbing his hands happily. "I have led you to civilization through the uncharted wastes of Hill House."

"We ought to make a practice of leaving every door wide open." Theodora glanced nervously over her shoulder. "I *hate* this wandering around in the dark."

"You'd have to prop them open with something, then,"

Eleanor said. "Every door in this house swings shut when you let go of it."

"Tomorrow," Dr. Montague said. "I will make a note. Door stops." He moved happily toward the sideboard, where Mrs. Dudley had set a warming oven and an impressive row of covered dishes. The table was set for four, with a lavish display of candles and damask and heavy silver.

"No stinting, I see," Luke said, taking up a fork with a gesture which would have confirmed his aunt's worst suspicions. "We get the company silver."

"I think Mrs. Dudley is proud of the house," Eleanor said.

"She doesn't intend to give us a poor table, at any rate," the doctor said, peering into the warming oven. "This is an excellent arrangement, I think. It gets Mrs. Dudley well away from here before dark and enables us to have our dinners without her uninviting company."

"Perhaps," Luke said, regarding the plate which he was filling generously, "perhaps I did good Mrs. Dudley—why *must* I continue to think of her, perversely, as *good* Mrs. Dudley?—perhaps I really did her an injustice. She said she hoped to find me alive in the morning, and our dinner was in the oven; now I suspect that she intended me to die of gluttony."

"What keeps her here?" Eleanor asked Dr. Montague. "Why do she and her husband stay on, alone in this house?"

"As I understand it, the Dudleys have taken care of Hill House ever since anyone can remember; certainly the Sandersons were happy enough to keep them on. But tomorrow—"

Theodora giggled. "Mrs. Dudley is probably the only true surviving member of the family to whom Hill House *really* belongs. *I* think she is only waiting until all the Sanderson heirs—that's you, Luke—die off in various horrible ways, and then she gets the house and the fortune in jewels buried in the cellar. Or maybe she and Dudley hoard their gold in the secret chamber, or there's oil under the house."

"There are no secret chambers in Hill House," the doctor said with finality. "Naturally, that possibility has been suggested before, and I think I may say with assurance that no such romantic devices exist here. But tomorrow—"

"In any case, oil is definitely old hat, nothing at all to discover on the property these days," Luke told Theodora. "The very least Mrs. Dudley could murder me for in cold blood is uranium."

"Or just the pure fun of it," Theodora said.

"Yes," Eleanor said, "but why are we here?"

For a long minute the three of them looked at her, Theodora and Luke curiously, the doctor gravely. Then Theodora said, "Just what *I* was going to ask. Why *are* we here? What *is* wrong with Hill House? What is going to happen?"

"Tomorrow—"

"No," Theodora said, almost petulantly. "We are three adult, intelligent people. We have all come a long way, Doctor Montague, to meet you here in Hill House; Eleanor wants to know why, and so do I."

"Me too," Luke said.

"Why did you bring us here, Doctor? Why are you here yourself? How did you hear about Hill House, and why does it have such a reputation and what really goes on here? What is going to *happen?*"

The doctor frowned unhappily. "I don't know," he said, and then, when Theodora made a quick, irritated gesture, he went on, "I know very little more about the house than you do, and naturally I intended to tell you everything I do know; as for what is going to *happen*, I will learn that when you do. But tomorrow is soon enough to talk about it, I think; daylight—"

"Not for me," Theodora said.

"I assure you," the doctor said, "that Hill House will be quiet tonight. There is a pattern to these things, as though psychic phenomena were subject to laws of a very particular sort."

"I really think we ought to talk it over tonight," Luke said.

"We're not afraid," Eleanor added.

The doctor sighed again. "Suppose," he said slowly, "you heard the story of Hill House and decided not to stay. How would you leave, tonight?" He looked around at them again, quickly. "The gates are locked. Hill House has a reputation for insistent hospitality; it seemingly dislikes letting its guests get away. The last person who tried to leave Hill House in darkness—it was eighteen years ago, I grant you—was killed at the turn in the driveway, where his horse bolted and crushed him against the big tree. Suppose I tell you about Hill House, and one of you wants to leave? Tomorrow, at least, we could see that you got safely to the village."

"But we're not going to run away," Theodora said. "I'm not, and Eleanor isn't, and Luke isn't."

"Stoutly, upon the ramparts," Luke agreed.

"You are a mutinous group of assistants. After dinner, then. We will retire to our little boudoir for coffee and a little of the good brandy Luke has in his suitcase, and I will tell you all I know about Hill House. Now, however, let us talk about music, or painting, or even politics."

4

"I had not decided," the doctor said, turning the brandy in his glass, "how best to prepare the three of you for Hill House. I certainly could not write you about it, and I am most unwilling now to influence your minds with its complete history before you have had a chance to see for yourselves." They were back in the small parlor, warm and almost sleepy. Theodora had abandoned any attempt at a chair and had put herself down on the hearthrug, cross-legged and drowsy. Eleanor, wanting to sit on the hearthrug beside her, had not thought of it in time and had condemned herself to one of the slippery chairs, unwilling now to attract attention by moving and getting herself awkwardly down onto the floor. Mrs. Dudley's good dinner and an hour's quiet conversation had evaporated the faint air of unreality and constraint; they had begun to know one another, recognize individual voices and mannerisms, faces and laughter; Eleanor thought with a little shock of surprise that she had been in Hill House only for four or five hours, and smiled a little at the fire. She could feel the thin stem of her glass between her fingers, the stiff pressure of the chair against her back, the faint movements of air through the room which were barely perceptible in small stirrings of tassels and beads. Darkness lay in the corners, and the marble cupid smiled down on them with chubby good humor.

"What a time for a ghost story," Theodora said.

"If you please." The doctor was stiff. "We are not children trying to frighten one another," he said.

"Sorry." Theodora smiled up at him. "I'm just trying to get myself used to all of this."

"Let us," said the doctor, "exercise great caution in our language. Preconceived notions of ghosts and apparitions—"

"The disembodied hand in the soup," Luke said helpfully.

"My dear boy. *If* you please. I was trying to explain that our purpose here, since it is of a scientific and exploratory nature, ought not to be affected, perhaps even warped, by half-remembered spooky stories which belong more properly to a—let me see—a marshmallow roast." Pleased with himself, he looked around to be sure that they were all amused. "As a matter of fact, my researches over the past few years have led me to certain theories regarding psychic phenomena which I have now, for the first time, an opportunity of testing. Ideally, of course, you ought not to know anything about Hill House. You should be ignorant and receptive."

"And take notes," Theodora murmured.

"Notes. Yes, indeed. Notes. However, I realize that it is most impractical to leave you entirely without background information, largely because you are not people accustomed to meeting a situation without preparation." He beamed at them slyly. "You are three willful, spoiled children who are prepared to nag me for your bedtime story." Theodora giggled, and the doctor nodded at her happily. He rose and moved to stand by the fire in an unmistakable classroom pose; he seemed to feel the lack of a blackboard behind him, because once or twice he half turned, hand raised, as though looking for chalk to illustrate a point. "Now," he said, "we will take up the history of Hill House." I wish I had a notebook and a pen, Eleanor thought, just to make him feel at home. She glanced at Theodora and Luke and found both their faces fallen instinctively into a completely rapt classroom look; high earnestness, she thought; we have moved into another stage of our adventure.

"You will recall," the doctor began, "the houses described in Leviticus as 'leprous,' *tsaraas*, or Homer's phrase for the underworld: *aidao domos*, the house of Hades; I need not remind you, I think, that the concept of certain houses as unclean or forbidden—perhaps sacred—is as old as the mind of man. Certainly there are spots which inevitably attach to themselves an atmosphere of holiness and goodness; it might not then be too fanciful to say that some houses are born bad. Hill House, whatever the cause, has been unfit for human habitation for upwards of twenty years. What it was like before then, whether its personality was molded by the people who lived here, or the things they did, or whether it was evil from its start are all questions I cannot answer. Naturally I hope that we will all know a good deal more about Hill House before we leave. No one knows, even, why some houses are called haunted."

"What else *could* you call Hill House?" Luke demanded.

"Well—disturbed, perhaps. Leprous. Sick. Any of the popular euphemisms for insanity; a deranged house is a pretty conceit. There are popular theories, however, which discount the eerie, the mysterious; there are people who will tell you that the disturbances I am calling 'psychic' are actually the result of subterranean waters, or electric currents, or hallucinations caused by polluted air; atmospheric pressure, sun spots, earth tremors all have their advocates among the skeptical. People," the doctor said sadly, "are always so anxious to get things out into the open where they can put a name to them, even a meaningless name, so long as it has something of a scientific ring." He sighed, relaxing, and gave them a little quizzical smile. "A haunted house," he said. "Everyone laughs. I found myself telling my colleagues at the university that I was going camping this summer."

"I told people I was participating in a scientific experiment," Theodora said helpfully. "Without telling them where or what, of course."

"Presumably your friends feel less strongly about scientific experiments than mine. Yes." The doctor sighed again. "Camping. At my age. And yet *that* they believed. Well." He straightened up again and fumbled at his side, perhaps for a yardstick. "I first heard about Hill House a year ago, from a former tenant. He began by assuring me that he had left Hill House because his family objected to living so far out in the country, and ended by saying that in his opinion the house ought to be burned down and the ground sowed with salt. I learned of other people who had rented Hill House, and found that none of them had stayed more than a few days, certainly never the full terms of their leases, giving reasons that ranged from the dampness of the location—not at all true, by the way; the house is very dry—

to a pressing need to move elsewhere, for business reasons. That is, every tenant who has left Hill House hastily has made an effort to supply a rational reason for leaving, and yet every one of them has left. I tried, of course, to learn more from these former tenants, and yet in no case could I persuade them to discuss the house; they all seemed most unwilling to give me information and were, in fact, reluctant to recall the details of their several stays. In only one opinion were they united. Without exception, every person who has spent any length of time in this house urged me to stay as far away from it as possible. Not one of the former tenants could bring himself to admit that Hill House was haunted, but when I visited Hillsdale and looked up the newspaper records—"

"Newspapers?" Theodora asked. "Was there a scandal?"

"Oh, yes," the doctor said. "A perfectly splendid scandal, with a suicide and madness and lawsuits. *Then* I learned that the local people had no doubts about the house. I heard a dozen different stories, of course—it is really *unbelievably* difficult to get accurate information about a haunted house; it would astonish you to know what I have gone through to learn only as much as I have—and as a result I went to Mrs. Sanderson, Luke's aunt, and arranged to rent Hill House. She was most frank about its undesirability—"

"It's harder to burn down a house than you think," Luke said.

"—but agreed to allow me a short lease to carry out my researches, on condition that a member of the family be one of my party."

"They hope," Luke said solemnly, "that I will dissuade you from digging up the lovely old scandals."

"There. Now I have explained how I happen to be here, and why Luke has come. As for you two ladies, we all know by now that you are here because I wrote you, and you accepted my invitation. I hoped that each of you might, in her own way, intensify the forces at work in the house; Theodora has shown herself possessed of some telepathic ability, and Eleanor has in the past been intimately involved in poltergeist phenomena—"

"*I?*"

"Of course." The doctor looked at her curiously. "Many years ago, when you were a child. The stones—"

Eleanor frowned, and shook her head. Her fingers trembled around the stem of her glass, and then she said, "That was the neighbors. My mother said the neighbors did that. People are always jealous."

"Perhaps so." The doctor spoke quietly and smiled at Eleanor. "The incident has been forgotten long ago, of course; I only mentioned it because that is why I wanted you in Hill House."

"When *I* was a child," Theodora said lazily, "—'many years ago,' Doctor, as you put it so tactfully—I was whipped for throwing a brick through a greenhouse roof. I remember I thought about it for a long time, remembering the whipping but remembering also the lovely crash, and after thinking about it very seriously I went out and did it again."

"I don't remember very well," Eleanor said uncertainly to the doctor.

"But *why?*" Theodora asked. "I mean, I can accept that Hill House is supposed to be haunted, and you want us here, Doctor Montague, to help keep track of what happens—and I bet besides that you wouldn't at all like being here *alone*—but I just don't understand. It's a horrible old house, and if I rented it I'd scream for my money back after one fast look at the front hall, but what's *here?* What really frightens people so?"

"I will not put a name to what has no name," the doctor said. "I don't know."

"They never even told me what was going on," Eleanor said urgently to the doctor. "My mother said it was the neighbors, they were always against us because she wouldn't mix with them. My mother—"

Luke interrupted her, slowly and deliberately. "I think," he said, "that what we all want is facts. Something we can understand and put together."

"First," the doctor said, "I am going to ask you all a question. Do you want to leave? Do you advise that we pack up now and leave Hill House to itself, and never have anything more to do with it?"

He looked at Eleanor, and Eleanor put her hands together tight; it is another chance to get away, she was thinking, and she said, "No," and glanced with embarrassment at Theodora. "I was kind of a baby this afternoon," she explained. "I did let myself get frightened."

"She's not telling all the truth," Theodora said loyally. "She wasn't any more frightened than I was; we scared each other to death over a rabbit."

"Horrible creatures, rabbits," Luke said.

The doctor laughed. "I suppose we were all nervous this afternoon, anyway. It is a rude shock to turn that corner and get a clear look at Hill House."

"I thought he was going to send the car into a tree," Luke said.

"I am really very brave now, in a warm room with a fire and company," Theodora said.

"I don't think we could leave now if we wanted to." Eleanor had spoken before she realized clearly what she was going to say, or what it was going to sound like to the others; she saw that they were staring at her, and laughed and added lamely, "Mrs. Dudley would never forgive us." She wondered if they really believed that that was what she had meant to say, and thought, Perhaps it has us now, this house, perhaps it will not let us go.

"Let us have a little more brandy," the doctor said, "and I will tell you the story of Hill House." He returned to his classroom position before the fireplace and began slowly, as one giving an account of kings long dead and wars long done with; his voice was carefully unemotional. "Hill House was built eighty-odd years ago," he began. "It was built as a home for his family by a man named Hugh Crain, a country home where he hoped to see his children and grandchildren live in comfortable luxury, and where he fully expected to end his days in quiet. Unfortunately Hill House was a sad house almost from the beginning; Hugh Crain's young wife died minutes before she first was to set eyes on the house, when the carriage bringing her here overturned in the driveway, and the lady was brought— ah, *lifeless*, I believe is the phrase they use—into the home her husband had built for her. He was a sad and bitter man, Hugh Crain, left with two small daughters to bring up, but he did not leave Hill House."

"Children grew up here?" Eleanor asked incredulously.

The doctor smiled. "The house is dry, as I said. There were no swamps to bring them fevers, the country air was thought to be beneficial to them, and the house itself was regarded as luxurious. I have no doubt that two small children could play here, lonely perhaps, but not unhappy."

"I hope they went wading in the brook," Theodora said. She stared deeply into the fire. "Poor little things. I hope someone let them run in that meadow and pick wild-flowers."

"Their father married again," the doctor went on. "Twice more, as a matter of fact. He seems to have been—unlucky in his wives. The second Mrs. Crain died of a fall, although I have been unable to ascertain how or why. Her death seems to have been as tragically unexpected as her predecessor's. The third Mrs. Crain died of what they used to call consumption, somewhere in Europe; there is, some-where in the library, a collection of postcards sent to the two little girls left behind in Hill House from their father and their stepmother traveling from one health resort to another. The little girls were left here with their governess until their stepmother's death. After that Hugh Crain de-clared his intention of closing Hill House and remaining abroad, and his daughters were sent to live with a cousin of their mother's, and there they remained until they were grown up."

"I hope Mama's cousin was a little jollier than old Hugh," Theodora said, still staring darkly into the fire. "It's not nice to think of children growing up like mushrooms, in the dark."

"They felt differently," the doctor said. "The two sisters spent the rest of their lives quarreling over Hill House. After all his high hopes of a dynasty centered here, Hugh Crain died somewhere in Europe, shortly after his wife, and Hill House was left jointly to the two sisters, who must have been quite young ladies by then; the older sister had, at any rate, made her debut into society."

"And put up her hair, and learned to drink champagne and carry a fan . . ."

"Hill House was empty for a number of years, but kept always in readiness for the family; at first in expectation of Hugh Crain's return, and then, after his death, for either of the sisters who chose to live there. Somewhere during this time it was apparently agreed between the two sisters that Hill House should become the property of the older; the younger sister had married—"

"Aha," Theodora said. "The *younger* sister married. Stole her sister's beau, I've no doubt."

"It was said that the older sister was crossed in love," the doctor agreed, "although that is said of almost any lady who prefers, for whatever reason, to live alone. At any rate, it was the older sister who came back here to live. She seems to have resembled her father strongly; she lived here alone for a number of years, almost in seclusion, although the village of Hillsdale knew her. Incredible as it may sound to you, she genuinely loved Hill House and looked upon it as her family home. She eventually took a girl from the village to live with her, as a kind of companion; so far as I can learn there seems to have been no strong feeling among the villagers about the house then, since old Miss Crain—as she was inevitably known—hired her servants in the village, and it was thought a fine thing for her to take the village girl as a companion. Old Miss Crain was in constant disagreement with her sister over the house, the younger sister insisting that she had given up her claim on the house in exchange for a number of family heirlooms, some of considerable value, which her sister then refused to give her. There were some jewels, several pieces of antique furniture, and a set of gold-rimmed dishes, which seemed to irritate the younger sister more than anything else. Mrs. Sanderson let me rummage through a box of family papers, and so I have seen some of the letters Miss Crain received from her sister, and in all of them those dishes stand out as the recurrent sore subject. At any rate, the older sister died of pneumonia here in the house, with only the little companion to help her—there were stories later of a doctor called too late, of the old lady lying neglected upstairs while the younger woman dallied in the garden with some village lout, but I suspect that these are only scandalous inventions; I certainly cannot find that anything of the sort was widely believed at the time, and in fact most of the stories seem to stem directly from the poisonous vengefulness of the younger sister, who never rested in her anger."

"I don't like the younger sister," Theodora said. "First she stole her sister's lover, and then she tried to steal her sister's dishes. No, I don't like her."

"Hill House has an impressive list of tragedies connected with it, but then, most old houses have. People have to live and die *somewhere*, after all, and a house can hardly stand for eighty years without seeing some of its inhabitants die within its walls. After the death of the older sister, there was a lawsuit over the house. The companion insisted that the house was left to her, but the younger sister and her husband maintained most violently that the house belonged legally to them and claimed that the companion had tricked the older sister into signing away property which she had always intended leaving to her sister. It was an unpleasant business, like all family quarrels, and as in all family quarrels incredibly harsh and cruel things were said on either side. The companion swore in court—and here, I think, is the first hint of Hill House in its true personality—that the younger sister came into the house at night and stole things. When she was pressed to enlarge upon this accusation, she became very nervous and incoherent, and finally, forced to give some evidence for her charge, said that a silver service was missing, and a valuable set of enamels, in addition to the famous set of gold-rimmed dishes, which would actually be a very difficult thing to steal, when you think about it. For her part, the younger sister went so far as to mention murder and demand an investigation into the death of old Miss Crain, bringing up the first hints of the stories of neglect and mismanagement. I cannot discover that these suggestions were ever taken seriously. There is no record whatever of any but the most formal notice of the older sister's death, and certainly the villagers would have been the first to wonder if there had been any oddness about the death. The companion won her case at last, and could, in my opinion, have won a case for slander besides, and the house became legally hers, although the younger sister never gave up trying to get it. She kept after the unfortunate companion with letters and threats, made the wildest accusations against her everywhere, and in the local police records there is listed at least one occasion when the com-

panion was forced to apply for police protection to prevent her enemy from attacking her with a broom. The
companion went in terror, seemingly; her house burgled
at night—she never stopped insisting that they came and
stole things—and I read one pathetic letter in which she
complained that she had not spent a peaceful night in the
house since the death of her benefactor. Oddly enough,
sympathy around the village was almost entirely with the
younger sister, perhaps because the companion, once a village girl, was now lady of the manor. The villagers believed
—and still believe, I think—that the younger sister was de-
frauded of her inheritance by a scheming young woman.
They did not believe that she would murder her friend,
you see, but they were delighted to believe that she was
dishonest, certainly because they were capable of dishonesty themselves when opportunity arose. Well, gossip is
always a bad enemy. When the poor creature killed herself—"

"Killed herself?" Eleanor, shocked into speech, half rose.
"She had to kill herself?"

"You mean, was there another way of escaping her tor-
mentor? She certainly did not seem to think so. It was accepted locally that she had chosen suicide because her guilty
conscience drove her to it. I am more inclined to believe
that she was one of those tenacious, unclever young women
who can hold on desperately to what they believe is their
own but cannot withstand, mentally, a constant nagging
persecution; she had certainly no weapons to fight back
against the younger sister's campaign of hatred, her own
friends in the village had been turned against her, and she

seems to have been maddened by the conviction that locks and bolts could not keep out the enemy who stole into her house at night—"

"She should have gone away," Eleanor said. "Left the house and run as far as she could go."

"In effect, she did. I really think the poor girl was hated to death; she hanged herself, by the way. Gossip says she hanged herself from the turret on the tower, but when you have a house like Hill House with a tower and a turret, gossip would hardly allow you to hang yourself anywhere else. After her death, the house passed legally into the hands of the Sanderson family, who were cousins of hers and in no way as vulnerable to the persecutions of the younger sister, who must have been a little demented herself by that time. I heard from Mrs. Sanderson that when the family— it would have been her husband's parents—first came to see the house, the younger sister showed up to abuse them, standing on the road to howl at them as they went by, and found herself packed right off to the local police station. And that seems to be the end of the younger sister's part in the story: from the day the first Sanderson sent her packing to the brief notice of her death a few years later, she seems to have spent her time brooding silently over her wrongs, but far away from the Sandersons. Oddly enough, in all her ranting, she insisted always on one point—she had not, would not, come into this house at night, to steal or for any other reason."

"Was anything ever really stolen?" Luke asked.

"As I told you, the companion was finally pressed into saying that one or two things seemed to be missing, but could not say for sure. As you can imagine, the story of the nightly intruder did a good deal to enhance Hill House's further reputation. Moreover, the Sandersons did not live here at all. They spent a few days in the house, telling the villagers that they were preparing it for their immediate occupancy, and then abruptly cleared out, closing the house the way it stood. They told around the village that urgent business took them to live in the city, but the villagers thought they knew better. No one has lived in the house since for more than a few days at a time. It has been on the market, for sale or rent, ever since. Well, that is a long story. I need more brandy."

"Those two poor little girls," Eleanor said, looking into the fire. "I can't forget them, walking through these dark rooms, trying to play dolls, maybe, in here or those bedrooms upstairs."

"And so the old house has just been sitting here." Luke put out a tentative finger and touched the marble cupid gingerly. "Nothing in it touched, nothing used, nothing here wanted by anyone any more, just sitting here thinking."

"And waiting," Eleanor said.

"And waiting," the doctor confirmed. "Essentially," he went on slowly, "the evil is the house itself, I think. It has enchained and destroyed its people and their lives, it is a place of contained ill will. Well. Tomorrow you will see it all. The Sandersons put in electricity and plumbing and a telephone when they first thought to live here, but otherwise nothing has been changed."

"Well," Luke said after a little silence, "I'm sure we will all be very comfortable here."

5

Eleanor found herself unexpectedly admiring her own feet. Theodora dreamed over the fire just beyond the tips of her toes, and Eleanor thought with deep satisfaction that her feet were handsome in their red sandals; what a complete and separate thing I am, she thought, going from my red toes to the top of my head, individually an I, possessed of attributes belonging only to me. I have red shoes, she thought—that goes with being Eleanor; I dislike lobster and sleep on my left side and crack my knuckles when I am nervous and save buttons. I am holding a brandy glass which is mine because I am here and I am using it and I have a place in this room. I have red shoes and tomorrow I will wake up and I will still be here.

"I have red shoes," she said very softly, and Theodora turned and smiled up at her.

"I *had* intended—" and the doctor looked around at them with bright, anxious optimism—"I *had* intended to ask if you all played bridge?"

"Of course," Eleanor said. I play bridge, she thought; I used to have a cat named Dancer; I can swim.

"I'm afraid not," Theodora said, and the other three turned and regarded her with frank dismay.

"Not at all?" the doctor asked.

"I've been playing bridge twice a week for eleven years," Eleanor said, "with my mother and her lawyer and his wife —I'm *sure* you must play as well as *that*."

"Maybe you could teach me?" Theodora asked. "I'm quick at learning games."

"Oh, dear," the doctor said, and Eleanor and Luke laughed.

"We'll do something else instead," Eleanor said; I can play bridge, she thought; I like apple pie with sour cream, and I drove here by myself.

"Backgammon," the doctor said with bitterness.

"I play a fair game of chess," Luke said to the doctor, who cheered at once.

Theodora set her mouth stubbornly. "I didn't suppose we came here to play *games*," she said.

"Relaxation," the doctor said vaguely, and Theodora turned with a sullen shrug and stared again into the fire.

"I'll get the chessmen, if you'll tell me where," Luke said, and the doctor smiled.

"Better let me go," he said. "I've studied a floor plan of the house, remember. If we let you go off wandering by yourself we'd very likely never find you again." As the door closed behind him Luke gave Theodora a quick curious glance and then came over to stand by Eleanor. "You're not nervous, are you? Did that story frighten you?"

Eleanor shook her head emphatically, and Luke said, "You looked pale."

"I probably ought to be in bed," Eleanor said. "I'm not used to driving as far as I did today."

"Brandy," Luke said. "It will make you sleep better. You too," he said to the back of Theodora's head.

"Thank you," Theodora said coldly, not turning. "I rarely have trouble sleeping."

Luke grinned knowingly at Eleanor, and then turned as the doctor opened the door. "My wild imagination," the doctor said, setting down the chess set. "What a house this is."

"Did something happen?" Eleanor asked.

The doctor shook his head. "We probably ought to agree, now, not to wander around the house alone," he said.

"What happened?" Eleanor asked.

"My own imagination," the doctor said firmly. "This table all right, Luke?"

"It's a lovely old chess set," Luke said. "I wonder how the younger sister happened to overlook it."

"I can tell you one thing," the doctor said, "if it *was* the younger sister sneaking around this house at night, she had nerves of iron. It watches," he added suddenly. "The house. It watches every move you make." And then, "My own imagination, of course."

In the light of the fire Theodora's face was stiff and sulky; she likes attention, Eleanor thought wisely and, without thinking, moved and sat on the floor beside Theodora. Behind her she could hear the gentle sound of chessmen being set down on a board and the comfortable small movements of Luke and the doctor taking each other's measure, and in the fire there were points of flame and little stirrings. She waited a minute for Theodora to speak, and then said agreeably, "Still hard to believe you're really here?"

"I had no idea it would be so dull," Theodora said.

"We'll find plenty to do in the morning," Eleanor said.

"At home there would be people around, and lots of talking and laughing and lights and excitement—"

"I suppose I don't need such things," Eleanor said, almost apologetically. "There never was much excitement for me. I had to stay with Mother, of course. And when she was asleep I kind of got used to playing solitaire or listening to the radio. I never could bear to read in the evenings because I had to read aloud to her for two hours every afternoon. Love stories"—and she smiled a little, looking into the fire. But that's not all, she thought, astonished at herself, that doesn't tell what it was like, even if I wanted to tell; why am I talking?

"I'm terrible, aren't I?" Theodora moved quickly and put her hand over Eleanor's. "I sit here and grouch because there's nothing to amuse me; I'm very selfish. Tell me how horrible I am." And in the firelight her eyes shone with delight.

"You're horrible," Eleanor said obediently; Theodora's hand on her own embarrassed her. She disliked being touched, and yet a small physical gesture seemed to be Theodora's chosen way of expressing contrition, or pleasure, or sympathy; I wonder if my fingernails are clean, Eleanor thought, and slid her hand away gently.

"I am horrible," Theodora said, good-humored again. "I'm horrible and beastly and no one can stand me. There. Now tell me about yourself."

"I'm horrible and beastly and no one can stand me."

Theodora laughed. "Don't make fun of me. You're sweet and pleasant and everyone likes you very much; Luke has fallen madly in love with you, and I am jealous. Now I want to know more about you. Did you really take care of your mother for many years?"

"Yes," Eleanor said. Her fingernails *were* dirty, and her hand was badly shaped and people made jokes about love because sometimes it was funny. "Eleven years, until she died three months ago."

"Were you sorry when she died? Should I say how sorry *I* am?"

"No. She wasn't very happy."

"And neither were you?"

"And neither was I."

"But what about now? What did you do afterward, when you were free at last?"

"I sold the house," Eleanor said. "My sister and I each took whatever we wanted from it, small things; there was really nothing much except little things my mother had saved—my father's watch, and some old jewelry. Not at all like the sisters of Hill House."

"And you sold everything else?"

"Everything. Just as soon as I could."

"And then of course you started a gay, mad fling that brought you inevitably to Hill House?"

"Not exactly." Eleanor laughed.

"But all those wasted years! Did you go on a cruise, look for exciting young men, buy new clothes . . . ?"

"Unfortunately," Eleanor said dryly, "there was not at all that much money. My sister put her share into the bank for her little girl's education. I did buy some clothes, to come to Hill House." People like answering questions about themselves, she thought; what an odd pleasure it is. I would answer anything right now.

"What will you do when you go back? Do you have a job?"

"No, no job right now. I don't know what I'm going to do."

"I know what *I'll* do." Theodora stretched luxuriously. "I'll turn on every light in our apartment and just bask."

"What is your apartment like?"

Theodora shrugged. "Nice," she said. "We found an old place and fixed it up ourselves. One big room, and a couple of small bedrooms, nice kitchen—we painted it red and white and made over a lot of old furniture we dug up in junk shops—one really nice table, with a marble top. We both love doing over old things."

"Are you married?" Eleanor asked.

There was a little silence, and then Theodora laughed quickly and said, "No."

"Sorry," Eleanor said, horribly embarrassed. "I didn't mean to be curious."

"You're funny," Theodora said and touched Eleanor's cheek with her finger. There are lines by my eyes, Eleanor thought, and turned her face away from the fire. "Tell me where you live," Theodora said.

Eleanor thought, looking down at her hands which were badly shaped. We could have afforded a laundress, she thought; it wasn't fair. My hands are awful. "I have a little place of my own," she said slowly. "An apartment, like yours, only I live alone. Smaller than yours, I'm sure. I'm still furnishing it—buying one thing at a time, you know, to make sure I get everything absolutely right. White curtains. I had to look for weeks before I found my little stone lions on each corner of the mantel, and I have a white cat and my books and records and pictures. Everything has to be exactly the way I want it, because there's only me to use it; once I had a blue cup with stars painted on the inside; when you looked down into a cup of tea it was full of stars. I want a cup like that."

"Maybe one will turn up someday, in my shop," Theodora said. "Then I can send it to you. Someday you'll get a little package saying 'To Eleanor with love from her friend Theodora,' and it will be a blue cup full of stars."

"I would have stolen those gold-rimmed dishes," Eleanor said, laughing.

"Mate," Luke said, and the doctor said, "Oh dear, oh dear."

"Blind luck," Luke said cheerfully. "Have you ladies fallen asleep there by the fire?"

"Just about," Theodora said. Luke came across the room and held out a hand to each of them to help them up, and Eleanor, moving awkwardly, almost fell; Theodora rose in a quick motion and stretched and yawned. "Theo is sleepy," she said.

"I'll have to lead you upstairs," the doctor said. "Tomorrow we must really start to learn our way around. Luke, will you screen the fire?"

"Had we better make sure that the doors are locked?" Luke asked. "I imagine that Mrs. Dudley locked the back door when she left, but what about the others?"

"I hardly think we'll catch anyone breaking in," Theodora said. "Anyway, the little companion used to lock her doors, and what good did it do her?"

"Suppose we want to break out?" Eleanor asked.

The doctor glanced quickly at Eleanor and then away. "I see no need for locking doors," he said quietly.

"There is certainly not much danger of burglars from the village," Luke said.

"In any case," the doctor said, "I will not sleep for an hour or so yet; at my age an hour's reading before bedtime is essential, and I wisely brought *Pamela* with me. If any of you has trouble sleeping, I will read aloud to you. I never yet knew anyone who could not fall asleep with Richardson being read aloud to him." Talking quietly, he led them down the narrow hallway and through the great front hall and to the stairs. "I have often planned to try it on very small children," he went on.

Eleanor followed Theodora up the stairs; she had not realized until now how worn she was, and each step was an effort. She reminded herself naggingly that she was in Hill House, but even the blue room meant only, right now, the bed with the blue coverlet and the blue quilt. "On the other hand," the doctor continued behind her, "a Fielding novel comparable in length, although hardly in subject matter, would never do for very young children. I even have doubts about Sterne—"

Theodora went to the door of the green room and turned and smiled. "If you feel the least bit nervous," she said to Eleanor, "run right into my room."

"I will," Eleanor said earnestly. "Thank you; good night."

"—and certainly not Smollett. Ladies, Luke and I are here, on the other side of the stairway—"

"What color are your rooms?" Eleanor asked, unable to resist.

"Yellow," the doctor said, surprised.

"Pink," Luke said with a dainty gesture of distaste.

"We're blue and green down here," Theodora said.

"I will be awake, reading," the doctor said. "I will leave my door ajar, so I will certainly hear any sound. Good night. Sleep well."

"Good night," Luke said. "Good night, all."

As she closed the door of the blue room behind her Eleanor thought wearily that it might be the darkness and oppression of Hill House that tired her so, and then it no longer mattered. The blue bed was unbelievably soft. Odd, she thought sleepily, that the house should be so dreadful and yet in many respects so physically comfortable—the soft bed, the pleasant lawn, the good fire, the cooking of Mrs. Dudley. The company too, she thought, and then thought, Now I can think about them; I am all alone. Why is Luke here? But why am *I* here? Journeys end in lovers meeting. They all saw that I was afraid.

She shivered and sat up in bed to reach for the quilt at the foot. Then, half amused and half cold, she slipped out of bed and went, barefoot and silent, across the room to turn the key in the lock of the door; they won't know I locked it, she thought, and went hastily back to bed. With the quilt pulled up around her she found herself looking with quick apprehension at the window, shining palely in the darkness, and then at the door. I wish I had a sleeping pill to take, she thought, and looked again over her shoulder, compulsively, at the window, and then again at the door, and thought, Is it moving? But I locked it; is it moving?

I think, she decided concretely, that I would like this better if I had the blankets over my head. Hidden deep in the bed under the blankets, she giggled and was glad none of the others could hear her. In the city she never slept with her head under the covers; I have come all this way today, she thought.

Then she slept, secure; in the next room Theodora slept,

smiling, with her light on. Farther down the hall the doctor, reading *Pamela*, lifted his head occasionally to listen, and once went to his door and stood for a minute, looking down the hall, before going back to his book. A nightlight shone at the top of the stairs over the pool of blackness which was the hall. Luke slept, on his bedside table a flashlight and the lucky piece he always carried with him. Around them the house brooded, settling and stirring with a movement that was almost like a shudder.

Six miles away Mrs. Dudley awakened, looked at her clock, thought of Hill House, and shut her eyes quickly. Mrs. Gloria Sanderson, who owned Hill House and lived three hundred miles away from it, closed her detective story, yawned, and reached up to turn off her light, wondering briefly if she had remembered to put the chain on the front door. Theodora's friend slept; so did the doctor's wife and Eleanor's sister. Far away, in the trees over Hill House, an owl cried out, and toward morning a thin, fine rain began, misty and dull.

~~~~~~

E LEANOR awakened to find the blue room gray
and colorless in the morning rain. She found that she had
thrown the quilt off during the night and had finished
sleeping in her usual manner, with her head on the pillow.
It was a surprise to find that she had slept until after
eight, and she thought that it was ironic that the first good
night's sleep she had had in years had come to her in Hill
House. Lying in the blue bed, looking up into the dim
ceiling with its remote carved pattern, she asked herself,

half asleep still, What did I do; did I make a fool of myself? Were they laughing at me?

Thinking quickly over the evening before, she could remember only that she had—must have—seemed foolishly, childishly contented, almost happy; had the others been amused to see that she was so simple? I said silly things, she told herself, and of course they noticed. Today I will be more reserved, less openly grateful to all of them for having me.

Then, awakening completely, she shook her head and sighed. You are a very silly baby, Eleanor, she told herself, as she did every morning.

The room came clearly alive around her; she was in the blue room at Hill House, the dimity curtains were moving slightly at the window, and the wild splashing in the bathroom must be Theodora, awake, sure to be dressed and ready first, certain to be hungry. "Good morning," Eleanor called, and Theodora answering, gasping, "Good morning—through in a minute—I'll leave the tub filled for you—are you starving? Because I am." Does she think I wouldn't bathe unless she left a full tub for me? Eleanor wondered, and then was ashamed; I came here to stop thinking things like that, she told herself sternly and rolled out of bed and went to the window. She looked out across the veranda roof to the wide lawn below, with its bushes and little clumps of trees wound around with mist. Far down at the end of the lawn was the line of trees which marked the path to the creek, although the prospect of a jolly picnic on the grass was not, this morning, so appealing. It was clearly going to be wet all day, but it was a summer rain, deepening the green of the grass and the trees, sweetening and cleaning the air. It's charming, Eleanor thought, surprised at herself; she wondered if she was the first person ever to find Hill House charming and then thought, chilled, Or do they *all* think so, the *first* morning? She shivered, and found herself at the same time unable to account for the excitement she felt, which made it difficult to remember why it was so odd to wake up happy in Hill House.

"I'll *starve* to death." Theodora pounded on the bathroom door, and Eleanor snatched at her robe and hurried. "Try to look like a stray sunbeam," Theodora called out from her room. "It's such a dark day we've got to be a little brighter than usual."

Sing before breakfast you'll cry before night, Eleanor told herself, because she had been singing softly, "In delay there lies no plenty. . . ."

"I thought *I* was the lazy one," Theodora said complacently through the door, "but you're much, *much* worse. Lazy hardly *begins* to describe you. You *must* be clean enough now to come and have breakfast."

"Mrs. Dudley sets out breakfast at nine. What will she think when we show up bright and smiling?"

"She will sob with disappointment. Did anyone scream for her in the night, do you suppose?"

Eleanor regarded a soapy leg critically. "I slept like a log," she said.

"So did I. If you are not ready in three minutes I will come in and drown you. I want my *breakfast*."

Eleanor was thinking that it had been a very long time since she had dressed to look like a stray sunbeam, or been so hungry for breakfast, or arisen so aware, so conscious of herself, so deliberate and tender in her attentions; she even brushed her teeth with a niceness she could not remember ever feeling before. It is all the result of a good night's sleep, she thought; since Mother died I must have been sleeping even more poorly than I realized.

"Aren't you ready *yet?*"

"Coming, coming," Eleanor said, and ran to the door, remembered that it was still locked, and unlocked it softly. Theodora was waiting for her in the hall, vivid in the dullness in gaudy plaid; looking at Theodora, it was not possible for Eleanor to believe that she ever dressed or washed or moved or ate or slept or talked without enjoying every minute of what she was doing; perhaps Theodora never cared at all what other people thought of her.

"Do you realize that we may be another hour or so just *finding* the dining room?" Theodora said. "But maybe they have left us a map—did you know that Luke and the doctor have been up for hours? I was talking to them from the window."

They have started without me, Eleanor thought; tomorrow I will wake up earlier and be there to talk from the window too. They came to the foot of the stairs, and Theodora crossed the great dark hall and put her hand confidently to a door. "Here," she said, but the door opened into a dim, echoing room neither of them had seen before. "Here," Eleanor said, but the door she chose led onto the narrow passage to the little parlor where last night they had sat before a fire.

"It's across the hall from *that*," Theodora said, and turned, baffled. "*Damn* it," she said, and put her head back and shouted. "Luke? Doctor?"

Distantly they heard an answering shout, and Theodora moved to open another door. "If they think," she said over her shoulder, "that they are going to keep me forever in this filthy hall, trying one door after another to get to my breakfast—"

"That's the right one, I think," Eleanor said, "with the dark room to go through, and then the dining room beyond."

Theodora shouted again, blundered against some light piece of furniture, cursed, and then the door beyond was opened and the doctor said, "Good morning."

"Foul, filthy house," Theodora said, rubbing her knee. "Good morning."

"You will never believe this now, of course," the doctor said, "but three minutes ago these doors were wide open. We left them open so you could find your way. We sat here and watched them swing shut just before you called. Well. Good morning."

"Kippers," Luke said from the table. "Good morning. I hope you ladies *are* the kipper kind."

They had come through the darkness of one night, they had met morning in Hill House, and they were a family, greeting one another with easy informality and going to the chairs they had used last night at dinner, their own places at the table.

"A fine big breakfast is what Mrs. Dudley certainly agreed to set out at nine," Luke said, waving a fork. "We had begun to wonder if you were the coffee-and-a-roll-in-bed types."

"We would have been here much sooner in any other house," Theodora said.

"Did you really leave all the doors open for us?" Eleanor asked.

"That's how we knew you were coming," Luke told her. "We saw the doors swing shut."

"Today we will nail all the doors open," Theodora said. "I am going to pace this house until I can find food ten times out of ten. I slept with my light on all night," she confided to the doctor, "but nothing happened at all."

"It was all very quiet," the doctor said.

"Did you watch over us all night?" Eleanor asked.

"Until about three, when *Pamela* finally put me to sleep. There wasn't a sound until the rain started sometime after two. One of you ladies called out in her sleep once—"

"That must have been me," Theodora said shamelessly. "Dreaming about the wicked sister at the gates of Hill House."

"I dreamed about her too," Eleanor said. She looked at the doctor and said suddenly, "It's *embarrassing*. To think about being afraid, I mean."

"We're all in it together, you know," Theodora said.

"It's worse if you try not to show it," the doctor said.

"Stuff yourself very full of kippers," Luke said. "Then it will be impossible to feel anything at all."

Eleanor felt, as she had the day before, that the conversation was being skillfully guided away from the thought of fear, so very present in her own mind. Perhaps she was to be allowed to speak occasionally for all of them so that, quieting her, they quieted themselves and could leave the subject behind them; perhaps, vehicle for every kind of fear, she contained enough for all. They are like children, she thought crossly, daring each other to go first, ready to turn and call names at whoever comes last; she pushed her plate away from her and sighed.

"Before I go to sleep *tonight*," Theodora was saying to the doctor, "I want to be sure that I have seen every inch of this house. No more lying there wondering what is over my head or under me. And we *have* to open some windows and keep the doors open and stop feeling our way around."

"Little signs," Luke suggested. "Arrows pointing, reading THIS WAY OUT."

"Or DEAD END," Eleanor said.

"Or WATCH OUT FOR FALLING FURNITURE," Theodora said. "*We*'ll make them," she said to Luke.

"First we all explore the house," Eleanor said, too quickly perhaps, because Theodora turned and looked at her curiously. "I don't want to find myself left behind in an attic or something," Eleanor added uncomfortably.

"No one wants to leave you behind anywhere," Theodora said.

"Then *I* suggest," Luke said, "that we first of all finish off the coffee in the pot, and then go nervously from room to room, endeavoring to discover some rational plan to this house, and leaving doors open as we go. I never thought," he said, shaking his head sadly, "that I would stand to inherit a house where I had to put up signs to find my way around."

"We need to find out what to call the rooms," Theodora said. "Suppose I told you, Luke, that I would meet you clandestinely in the second-best drawing room—how would you ever know where to find me?"

"You could keep whistling till I got there," Luke offered.

Theodora shuddered. "You would hear me whistling,

and calling you, while you wandered from door to door, never opening the right one, and I would be inside, not able to find any way to get out—"

"And nothing to eat," Eleanor said unkindly.

Theodora looked at her again. "And nothing to eat," she agreed after a minute. Then, "It's the crazy house at the carnival," she said. "Rooms opening out of each other and doors going everywhere at once and swinging shut when you come, and I bet that somewhere there are mirrors that make you look all sideways and an air hose to blow up your skirts, and something that comes out of a dark passage and laughs in your face—" She was suddenly quiet and picked up her cup so quickly that her coffee spilled.

"Not as bad as all that," the doctor said easily. "Actually, the ground floor is laid out in what I might almost call concentric circles of rooms; at the center is the little parlor where we sat last night; around it, roughly, are a series of rooms—the billiard room, for instance, and a dismal little den entirely furnished in rose-colored satin—"

"Where Eleanor and I will go each morning with our needlework."

"—and surrounding these—I call them the inside rooms because they are the ones with no direct way to the outside; they have no windows, you remember—surrounding these are the ring of outside rooms, the drawing room, the library, the conservatory, the—"

"No," Theodora said, shaking her head. "I am still lost back in the rose-colored satin."

"And the veranda goes all around the house. There are doors opening onto the veranda from the drawing room, and the conservatory, and one sitting room. There is also a passage—"

"Stop, stop." Theodora was laughing, but she shook her head. "It's a filthy, *rotten* house."

The swinging door in the corner of the dining room opened, and Mrs. Dudley stood, one hand holding the door open, looking without expression at the breakfast table. "I clear off at ten," Mrs. Dudley said.

"Good morning, Mrs. Dudley," Luke said.

Mrs. Dudley turned her eyes to him. "I clear off at ten," she said. "The dishes are supposed to be back on the shelves. I take them out again for lunch. I set out lunch at one, but first the dishes have to be back on the shelves."

"Of course, Mrs. Dudley." The doctor rose and put down his napkin. "Everybody ready?" he asked.

Under Mrs. Dudley's eye Theodora deliberately lifted her cup and finished the last of her coffee, then touched her mouth with her napkin and sat back. "Splendid breakfast," she said conversationally. "Do the dishes belong to the house?"

"They belong on the shelves," Mrs. Dudley said.

"And the glassware and the silver and the linen? Lovely old things."

"The linen," Mrs. Dudley said, "belongs in the linen drawers in the dining room. The silver belongs in the silver chest. The glasses belong on the shelves."

"We must be quite a bother to you," Theodora said.

Mrs. Dudley was silent. Finally she said, "I clear up at ten. I set out lunch at one."

Theodora laughed and rose. "On," she said, "on, on. Let us go and open doors."

They began reasonably enough with the dining-room door, which they propped open with a heavy chair. The room beyond was the game room; the table against which Theodora had stumbled was a low inlaid chess table ("Now, I could not have overlooked that last night," the doctor said irritably), and at one end of the room were card tables and chairs, and a tall cabinet where the chessmen had been, with croquet balls and the cribbage board.

"Jolly spot to spend a carefree hour," Luke said, standing in the doorway regarding the bleak room. The cold greens of the table tops were reflected unhappily in the dark tiles around the fireplace; the inevitable wood paneling was, here, not at all enlivened by a series of sporting prints which seemed entirely devoted to various methods of doing wild animals to death, and over the mantel a deerhead looked down upon them in patent embarrassment.

"This is where they came to enjoy themselves," Theodora said, and her voice echoed shakily from the high ceiling. "They came here," she explained, "to relax from the oppressive atmosphere of the rest of the house." The deerhead looked down on her mournfully. "Those two little girls," she said. "Can we *please* take down that *beast* up there?"

"I think it's taken a fancy to you," Luke said. "It's never taken its eyes off you since you came in. Let's get out of here."

They propped the door open as they left, and came out into the hall, which shone dully under the light from the open rooms. "When we find a room with a window," the doctor remarked, "we will open it; until then, let us be content with opening the front door."

"You keep thinking of the little children," Eleanor said to Theodora, "but I can't forget that lonely little companion, walking around these rooms, wondering who else was in the house."

Luke tugged the great front door open and wheeled the big vase to hold it; "Fresh air," he said thankfully. The warm smell of rain and wet grass swept into the hall, and for a minute they stood in the open doorway, breathing air from outside Hill House. Then the doctor said, "Now *here* is something none of you anticipated," and he opened a small door tucked in beside the tall front door and stood back, smiling. "The library," he said. "In the tower."

"I can't go in there," Eleanor said, surprising herself, but she could not. She backed away, overwhelmed with the cold air of mold and earth which rushed at her. "My mother—" she said, not knowing what she wanted to tell them, and pressed herself against the wall.

"Indeed?" said the doctor, regarding her with interest. "Theodora?" Theodora shrugged and stepped into the library; Eleanor shivered. "Luke?" said the doctor, but Luke was already inside. From where she stood Eleanor could see only a part of the circular wall of the library, with a narrow iron staircase going up and perhaps, since it was the tower, up and up and up; Eleanor shut her eyes, hearing the doctor's voice distantly, hollow against the stone of the library walls.

"Can you see the little trapdoor up there in the shadows?" he was asking. "It leads out onto a little balcony, and of course that's where she is commonly supposed to have hanged herself—the girl, you remember. A most suitable spot, certainly; more suitable for suicides, I would think, than for books. She is supposed to have tied the rope onto the iron railing and then just stepped—"

"Thanks," Theodora said from within. "I can visualize it perfectly, thank you. For myself, I would probably have anchored the rope onto the deer head in the game room, but I suppose she had some sentimental attachment to the tower; what a nice word 'attachment' is in that context, don't you think?"

"Delicious." It was Luke's voice, louder; they were coming out of the library and back to the hall where Eleanor waited. "I think that I will make this room into a night club. I will put the orchestra up there on the balcony, and dancing girls will come down that winding iron staircase; the bar—"

"Eleanor," Theodora said, "are you all right now? It's a perfectly awful room, and you were right to stay out of it."

Eleanor stood away from the wall; her hands were cold and she wanted to cry, but she turned her back to the library door, which the doctor propped open with a stack of books. "I don't think I'll do much reading while I'm here," she said, trying to speak lightly. "Not if the books smell like the library."

"I hadn't noticed a smell," the doctor said. He looked inquiringly at Luke, who shook his head. "Odd," the doctor went on, "and just the kind of thing we're looking for. Make a note of it, my dear, and try to describe it exactly."

Theodora was puzzled. She stood in the hallway, turning, looking back of her at the staircase and then around again at the front door. "Are there two front doors?" she asked. "Am I just mixed up?"

The doctor smiled happily; he had clearly been hoping

for some such question. "This is the only front door," he said. "It is the one you came in yesterday."

Theodora frowned. "Then why can't Eleanor and I see the tower from our bedroom windows? Our rooms look out over the front of the house, and yet—"

The doctor laughed and clapped his hands. "At last," he said. "Clever Theodora. This is why I wanted you to see the house by day. Come, sit on the stairs while I tell you."

Obediently they settled on the stairs, looking up at the doctor, who took on his lecturing stance and began formally, "One of the peculiar traits of Hill House is its design—"

"Crazy house at the carnival."

"Precisely. Have you not wondered at our *extreme* difficulty in finding our way around? An ordinary house would not have had the four of us in such confusion for so long, and yet time after time we choose the wrong doors, the room we want eludes us. Even I have had my troubles." He sighed and nodded. "I daresay," he went on, "that old Hugh Crain expected that someday Hill House might become a showplace, like the Winchester House in California or the many octagon houses; he designed Hill House himself, remember, and, I have told you before, he was a strange man. Every angle"—and the doctor gestured toward the doorway—"every angle is slightly wrong. Hugh Crain must have detested other people and their sensible squared-away houses, because he made his house to suit his mind. Angles which you assume are the right angles you are accustomed to, and have every right to expect are true, are actually a fraction of a degree off in one direction or another. I am sure, for instance, that you believe that the stairs you are sitting on are level, because you are not prepared for stairs which are not level—"

They moved uneasily, and Theodora put out a quick hand to take hold of the balustrade, as though she felt she might be falling.

"—are actually on a very slight slant toward the central shaft; the doorways are all a very little bit off center— that may be, by the way, the reason the doors swing shut unless they are held; I wondered this morning whether the approaching footsteps of you two ladies upset the delicate balance of the doors. Of course the result of all these tiny aberrations of measurement adds up to a fairly large dis- tortion in the house as a whole. Theodora cannot see the tower from her bedroom window because the tower actually stands at the corner of the house. From Theodora's bedroom window it is completely invisible, although from here it seems to be directly outside her room. The window of Theodora's room is actually fifteen feet to the left of where we are now."

Theodora spread her hands helplessly. "Golly," she said.

"I see," Eleanor said. "The veranda roof is what misleads us. I can look out my window and see the veranda roof and because I came directly into the house and up the stairs I assumed that the front door was right below, although really—"

"You see only the veranda roof," the doctor said. "The front door is far away; it and the tower are visible from the nursery, which is the big room at the end of the hall- way; we will see it later today. It is"—and his voice was saddened—"a masterpiece of architectural misdirection. The double stairway at Chambord—"

"Then everything is a little bit off center?" Theodora asked uncertainly. "That's why it all feels so disjointed?"

"What happens when you go back to a real house?" Eleanor asked. "I mean—a—well—a *real* house?"

"It must be like coming off shipboard," Luke said. "After being here for a while your sense of balance could be so distorted that it would take you a while to lose your sea legs, or your Hill House legs. Could it be," he asked the doctor, "that what people have been assuming were supernatural manifestations were really only the result of a slight loss of balance in the people who live here? The inner ear," he told Theodora wisely.

"It must certainly affect people in some way," the doctor said. "We have grown to trust blindly in our senses of balance and reason, and I can see where the mind might fight wildly to preserve its own familiar stable patterns against all evidence that it was leaning sideways." He turned away. "We have marvels still before us," he said, and they came down from the stairway and followed him, walking gingerly, testing the floors as they moved. They went down the narrow passage to the little parlor where they had sat the night before, and from there, leaving doors propped open behind them, they moved into the outer circle of rooms, which looked out onto the veranda. They pulled heavy draperies away from windows and the light from outside came into Hill House. They passed through a music room where a harp stood sternly apart from them, with never a jangle of strings to mark their footfalls. A grand piano stood tightly shut, with a candelabra above, no candle ever touched by flame. A marble-topped table held wax flowers under glass, and the chairs were twig-thin and gilded. Beyond this was the conservatory, with tall glass doors showing them the rain outside, and ferns growing damply around and over wicker furniture. Here it was uncomfortably moist, and they left it quickly, to come through an arched doorway into the drawing room and stand, aghast and incredulous.

"It's not there," Theodora said, weak and laughing. "I don't believe it's there." She shook her head. "Eleanor, do you see it too?"

"How . . . ?" Eleanor said helplessly.

"I thought you would be pleased." The doctor was complacent.

One entire end of the drawing room was in possession of a marble statuary piece; against the mauve stripes and flowered carpet it was huge and grotesque and somehow whitely naked; Eleanor put her hands over her eyes, and Theodora clung to her. "I thought it might be intended for Venus rising from the waves," the doctor said.

"Not at all," said Luke, finding his voice, "it's Saint Francis curing the lepers."

"No, no," Eleanor said. "One of them is a dragon."

"It's none of that," said Theodora roundly; "it's a family portrait, you sillies. Composite. *Any*one would know it at once; that figure in the center, that tall, undraped—good heavens!—masculine one, that's old Hugh, patting himself on the back because he built Hill House, and his two attendant nymphs are his daughters. The one on the right who seems to be brandishing an ear of corn is actually telling about her lawsuit, and the other one, the little one on the end, is the companion, and the one on the *other* end—"

"Is Mrs. Dudley, done from life," Luke said.

"And that grass stuff they're all standing on is really supposed to be the dining-room carpet, grown up a little. Did anyone else notice that dining-room carpet? It looks like a field of hay, and you can feel it tickling your ankles. In back, that kind of overspreading apple-tree kind of thing, *that*'s—"

"A symbol of the protection of the house, surely," Dr. Montague said.

"I'd hate to think it might fall on us," Eleanor said. "Since the house is so unbalanced, Doctor, isn't there some chance of that?"

"I have read that the statue was carefully, and at great expense, constructed to offset the uncertainty of the floor on which it stands. It was put in, at any rate, when the house was built, and it has not fallen yet. It is possible, you know, that Hugh Crain admired it, even found it lovely."

"It is also possible that he used it to scare his children with," Theodora said. "What a pretty room this would be without it." She turned, swinging. "A dancing room," she said, "for ladies in full skirts, and room enough for a full country dance. Hugh Crain, will you take a turn with me?" and she curtsied to the statue.

"I believe he's going to accept," Eleanor said, taking an involuntary step backward.

"Don't let him tread on your toes," the doctor said, and laughed. "Remember what happened to Don Juan."

Theodora touched the statue timidly, putting her finger against the outstretched hand of one of the figures. "Marble is always a shock," she said. "It never feels like you think it's going to. I suppose a lifesize statue looks enough like a real person to make you expect to feel skin." Then, turning again, and shimmering in the dim room, she waltzed alone, turning to bow to the statue.

"At the end of the room," the doctor said to Eleanor and Luke, "under those draperies, are doors leading onto the veranda; when Theodora is heated from dancing she may step out into the cooler air." He went the length of the room to pull aside the heavy blue draperies and opened the doors. Again the smell of the warm rain came in, and a burst of wind, so that a little breath seemed to move across the statue, and light touched the colored walls.

"Nothing in this house moves," Eleanor said, "until you look away, and then you just catch something from the corner of your eye. Look at the little figurines on the shelves; when we all had our backs turned they were dancing with Theodora."

"*I* move," Theodora said, circling toward them.

"Flowers under glass," Luke said. "Tassels. I am beginning to fancy this house."

Theodora pulled at Eleanor's hair. "Race you around the veranda," she said and darted for the doors. Eleanor, with no time for hesitation or thought, followed, and they ran out onto the veranda. Eleanor, running and laughing, came around a curve of the veranda to find Theodora going in another door, and stopped, breathless. They had come to the kitchen, and Mrs. Dudley, turning away from the sink, watched them silently.

"Mrs. Dudley," Theodora said politely, "we've been exploring the house."

Mrs. Dudley's eyes moved to the clock on the shelf over the stove. "It is half-past eleven," she said. "I—"

"—set lunch on at one," Theodora said. "We'd like to

look over the kitchen, if we may. We've seen all the other downstairs rooms, I think."

Mrs. Dudley was still for a minute and then, moving her head acquiescently, turned and walked deliberately across the kitchen to a farther doorway. When she opened it they could see the back stairs beyond, and Mrs. Dudley turned and closed the door behind her before she started up. Theodora cocked her head at the doorway and waited a minute before she said, "I wonder if Mrs. Dudley has a soft spot in her heart for me, I really do."

"I suppose she's gone up to hang herself from the turret," Eleanor said. "Let's see what's for lunch while we're here."

"Don't joggle anything," Theodora said. "You know perfectly well that the dishes belong on the shelves. Do you think that woman really means to make us a soufflé? Here is certainly a soufflé dish, and eggs and cheese—"

"It's a nice kitchen," Eleanor said. "In my mother's house the kitchen was dark and narrow, and nothing you cooked there ever had any taste or color."

"What about your own kitchen?" Theodora asked absently. "In your little apartment? Eleanor, look at the doors."

"I can't make a soufflé," Eleanor said.

"Look, Eleanor. There's the door onto the veranda, and another that opens onto steps going down—to the cellar, I guess—and another over there going onto the veranda again, and the one she used to go upstairs, and another one over there—"

"To the veranda again," Eleanor said, opening it. "Three doors going out onto the veranda from one kitchen."

"And the door to the butler's pantry and on into the dining room. Our good Mrs. Dudley likes doors, doesn't she? She can certainly"—and their eyes met—"get out fast in any direction if she wants to."

Eleanor turned abruptly and went back to the veranda. "I wonder if she had Dudley cut extra doors for her. I wonder how she likes working in a kitchen where a door in back of her might open without her knowing it. I wonder, actually, just what Mrs. Dudley is in the habit of meeting in her kitchen so that she wants to make sure that she'll find a way out no matter which direction she runs. I wonder—"

"Shut up," Theodora said amiably. "A nervous cook can't make a good soufflé, anyone knows that, and she's probably listening on the stairs. Let us choose one of her doors and leave it open behind us."

Luke and the doctor were standing on the veranda, looking out over the lawn; the front door was oddly close, beyond them. Behind the house, seeming almost overhead, the great hills were muted and dull in the rain. Eleanor wandered along the veranda, thinking that she had never before known a house so completely surrounded. Like a very tight belt, she thought; would the house fly apart if the veranda came off? She went what she thought must be the great part of the circle around the house, and then she saw the tower. It rose up before her suddenly, almost without warning, as she came around the curve of the veranda. It was made of gray stone, grotesquely solid, jammed hard against the wooden side of the house, with the insistent veranda holding it there. Hideous, she thought, and then thought that if the house burned away someday the tower would still stand, gray and forbidding over the ruins, warning people away from what was left of Hill House, with perhaps a stone fallen here and there, so owls and bats might fly in and out and nest among the books below. Halfway up windows began, thin angled slits in the stone, and she wondered what it would be like, looking down from them, and wondered that she had not been able to enter the tower. I will never look down from those windows, she thought, and tried to imagine the narrow iron stairway going up and around inside. High on top was a conical wooden roof, topped by a wooden spire. It must have been laughable in any other house, but here in Hill House it belonged, gleeful and expectant, awaiting perhaps a slight creature creeping out from the little window onto the slanted roof, reaching up to the spire, knotting a rope. . . .

"You'll fall," Luke said, and Eleanor gasped; she brought her eyes down with an effort and found that she was griping the veranda rail tightly and leaning far backward. "Don't trust your balance in my charming Hill House," Luke said, and Eleanor breathed deeply, dizzy, and staggered. He caught her and held her while she tried to steady herself in the rocking world where the trees and the lawn seemed somehow tilted sideways and the sky turned and swung.

"Eleanor?" Theodora said nearby, and she heard the sound of the doctor's feet running along the veranda. "This damnable house," Luke said. "You have to watch it every minute."

"Eleanor?" said the doctor.

"I'm all right," Eleanor said, shaking her head and standing unsteadily by herself. "I was leaning back to see the top of the tower and I got dizzy."

"She was standing almost sideways when I caught her," Luke said.

"I've had that feeling once or twice this morning," Theodora said, "as though I was walking up the wall."

"Bring her back inside," the doctor said. "It's not so bad when you're *inside* the house."

"I'm really all right," Eleanor said, very much embarrassed, and she walked with deliberate steps along the veranda to the front door, which was closed. "I thought we left it open," she said with a little shake in her voice, and the doctor came past her and pushed the heavy door open again. Inside, the hall had returned to itself; all the doors they had left open were neatly closed. When the doctor opened the door into the game room they could see beyond him that the doors to the dining room were closed, and the little stool they had used to prop one door open was neatly back in place against the wall. In the boudoir and the drawing room, the parlor and the conservatory, the doors and windows were closed, the draperies pulled together, and the darkness back again.

"It's Mrs. Dudley," Theodora said, trailing after the doctor and Luke, who moved quickly from one room to the next, pushing doors wide open again and propping them, sweeping drapes away from windows and letting in the warm, wet air. "Mrs. Dudley did it yesterday, as soon as Eleanor and I were out of the way, because she'd rather shut them herself than come along and find them shut by themselves because the doors belong shut and the windows belong shut and the dishes belong—" She began to laugh foolishly, and the doctor turned and frowned at her with irritation.

"Mrs. Dudley had better learn her place," he said. "I will nail these doors open if I have to." He turned down the passageway to their little parlor and sent the door swinging open with a crash. "Losing my temper will not help," he said, and gave the door a vicious kick.

"Sherry in the parlor before lunch," Luke said amiably. "Ladies, enter."

2

"Mrs. Dudley," the doctor said, putting down his fork, "an admirable soufflé."

Mrs. Dudley turned to regard him briefly and went into the kitchen with an empty dish.

The doctor sighed and moved his shoulders tiredly. "After my vigil last night, I feel the need of a rest this afternoon, and you," he said to Eleanor, "would do well to lie down for an hour. Perhaps a regular afternoon rest might be more comfortable for all of us."

"I see," said Theodora, amused. "I must take an afternoon nap. It may look funny when I go home again, but I can always tell them that it was part of my schedule at Hill House."

"Perhaps we will have trouble sleeping at night," the doctor said, and a little chill went around the table, darkening the light of the silver and the bright colors of the china, a little cloud that drifted through the dining room and brought Mrs. Dudley after it.

"It's five minutes of two," Mrs. Dudley said.

3

Eleanor did not sleep during the afternoon, although she would have liked to; instead, she lay on Theodora's bed in the green room and watched Theodora do her nails, chatting lazily, unwilling to let herself perceive that she had followed Theodora into the green room because she had not dared to be alone.

"I love decorating myself," Theodora said, regarding her hand affectionately. "I'd like to paint myself all over."

Eleanor moved comfortably. "Gold paint," she suggested, hardly thinking. With her eyes almost closed she could see Theodora only as a mass of color sitting on the floor.

"Nail polish and perfume and bath salts," Theodora said, as one telling the cities of the Nile. "Mascara. You don't think half enough of such things, Eleanor."

Eleanor laughed and closed her eyes altogether. "No time," she said.

"Well," Theodora said with determination, "by the time I'm through with you, you will be a different person; I dislike being with women of no color." She laughed to show that she was teasing, and then went on, "I think I will put red polish on your toes."

Eleanor laughed too and held out her bare foot. After a minute, nearly asleep, she felt the odd cold little touch of the brush on her toes, and shivered.

"Surely a famous courtesan like yourself is accustomed to the ministrations of handmaidens," Theodora said. "Your feet are dirty."

Shocked, Eleanor sat up and looked; her feet *were* dirty,

and her nails were painted bright red. "It's *horrible*," she said to Theodora, "it's *wicked*," wanting to cry. Then, helplessly, she began to laugh at the look on Theodora's face. "I'll go and wash my feet," she said.

"Golly." Theodora sat on the floor beside the bed, staring. "Look," she said. "My feet are dirty, too, baby, honest. *Look*."

"Anyway," Eleanor said, "I hate having things done to me."

"You're about as crazy as anyone *I* ever saw," Theodora said cheerfully.

"I don't like to feel helpless," Eleanor said. "My mother—"

"Your mother would have been delighted to see you with your toenails painted red," Theodora said. "They look nice."

Eleanor looked at her feet again. "It's wicked," she said inadequately. "I mean—on *my* feet. It makes me feel like I look like a fool."

"You've got foolishness and wickedness somehow mixed up." Theodora began to gather her equipment together. "Anyway, I won't take it off and we'll both watch to see whether Luke and the doctor look at your feet first."

"No matter what I try to say, you make it sound foolish," Eleanor said.

"Or wicked." Theodora looked up at her gravely. "I have a hunch," she said, "that you ought to go home, Eleanor."

Is she laughing at me? Eleanor wondered; has she decided that I am not fit to stay? "I don't want to go," she said, and Theodora looked at her again quickly and then away, and touched Eleanor's toes softly. "The polish is dry," she said. "I'm an idiot. Just something frightened me for a minute." She stood up and stretched. "Let's go look for the others," she said.

4

Luke leaned himself wearily against the wall of the upstairs hall, his head resting against the gold frame of an engraving of a ruin. "I keep thinking of this house as my own future property," he said, "more now than I did before; I keep telling myself that it will belong to me someday, and I keep asking myself why." He gestured at the length of the hall. "If I had a passion for doors," he said, "or gilded clocks, or miniatures; if I wanted a Turkish corner of my own, I would very likely regard Hill House as a fairyland of beauty."

"It's a handsome house," the doctor said stanchly. "It must have been thought of as elegant when it was built." He started off down the hall, to the large room on the end which had once been the nursery. "Now," he said, "we shall see the tower from a window"—and shivered as he passed through the door. Then he turned and looked back curiously. "Could there be a draft across that doorway?"

"A draft? In Hill House?" Theodora laughed. "Not unless you could manage to make one of those doors stay open."

"Come here one at a time, then," the doctor said, and Theodora moved forward, grimacing as she passed the doorway.

"Like the doorway of a tomb," she said. "It's warm enough inside, though."

Luke came, hesitated in the cold spot, and then moved quickly to get out of it, and Eleanor, following, felt with incredulity the piercing cold that struck her between one step and the next; it was like passing through a wall of ice, she thought, and asked the doctor, "What is it?"

The doctor was patting his hands together with delight. "You can keep your Turkish corners, my boy," he said. He reached out a hand and held it carefully over the location of the cold. "They *cannot* explain this," he said. "The very essence of the tomb, as Theodora points out. The cold spot in Borley Rectory only dropped eleven degrees," he went on complacently. "This, I should think, is considerably colder. The heart of the house."

Theodora and Eleanor had moved to stand closer together; although the nursery was warm, it smelled musty and close, and the cold crossing the doorway was almost tangible, visible as a barrier which must be crossed in order to get out. Beyond the windows the gray stone of the tower pressed close; inside, the room was dark and the line of nursery animals painted along the wall seemed somehow not at all jolly, but as though they were trapped, or related to the dying deer in the sporting prints of the game room. The nursery, larger than the other bedrooms, had an indefinable air of neglect found nowhere else in Hill House, and it crossed Eleanor's mind that even Mrs. Dudley's diligent care might not bring her across that cold barrier any oftener than necessary.

Luke had stepped back across the cold spot and was examining the hall carpet, then the walls, patting at the surfaces as though hoping to discover some cause for the odd cold. "It *couldn't* be a draft," he said, looking up at the doctor. "Unless they've got a direct air line to the North Pole. Everything's solid, anyway."

"I wonder who slept in the nursery," the doctor said irrelevantly. "Do you suppose they shut it up, once the children were gone?"

"Look," Luke said, pointing. In either corner of the hall, over the nursery doorway, two grinning heads were set; meant, apparently, as gay decorations for the nursery entrance, they were no more jolly or carefree than the animals inside. Their separate stares, captured forever in distorted laughter, met and locked at the point of the hall where the vicious cold centered. "When you stand where they can look at you," Luke explained, "they freeze you."

Curiously, the doctor stepped down the hall to join him, looking up. "Don't leave us alone in here," Theodora said, and ran out of the nursery, pulling Eleanor through the cold, which was like a fast slap, or a close cold breath. "A fine place to chill our beer," she said, and put out her tongue at the grinning faces.

"I must make a full account of this," the doctor said happily.

"It doesn't seem like an *impartial* cold," Eleanor said, awkward because she was not quite sure what she meant. "I felt it as *deliberate*, as though something wanted to give me an unpleasant shock."

"It's because of the faces, I suppose," the doctor said; he was on his hands and knees, feeling along the floor. "Measuring tape and thermometer," he told himself, "chalk for an outline; perhaps the cold intensifies at night? Everything is worse," he said, looking at Eleanor, "if you think something is looking at you."

Luke stepped through the cold, with a shiver, and closed the door to the nursery; he came back to the others in the hall with a kind of leap, as though he thought he could escape the cold by not touching the floor. With the nursery door closed they realized all at once how much darker it had become, and Theodora said restlessly, "Let's get downstairs to our parlor; I can feel those hills pushing in."

"After five," Luke said. "Cocktail time. I suppose," he said to the doctor, "you will trust me to mix you a cocktail again tonight?"

"Too much vermouth," the doctor said, and followed them lingeringly, watching the nursery door over his shoulder.

5

"I propose," the doctor said, setting down his napkin, "that we take our coffee in our little parlor. I find that fire very cheerful."

Theodora giggled. "Mrs. Dudley's gone, so let's race around fast and get all those doors and windows open and take everything down from the shelves—"

"The house seems different when she's not in it," Eleanor said.

"Emptier." Luke looked at her and nodded; he was arranging the coffee cups on a tray, and the doctor had already gone on, doggedly opening doors and propping them. "Each night I realize suddenly that we four are alone here."

"Although Mrs. Dudley's not much good as far as company is concerned; it's funny," Eleanor said, looking down at the dinner table, "I dislike Mrs. Dudley as much as any of you, but my mother would *never* let me get up and leave a table looking like this until morning."

"If she wants to leave before dark she has to clear away in the morning," Theodora said without interest. "*I'm* certainly not going to do it."

"It's not nice to walk away and leave a dirty table."

"You couldn't get them back on the right shelves anyway, and she'd have to do it all over again just to get your fingermarks off things."

"If I just took the silverware and let it soak—"

"No," Theodora said, catching her hand. "Do you want to go out into that kitchen all alone, with all those doors?"

"No," Eleanor said, setting down the handful of forks she had gathered. "I guess I don't, really." She lingered to look uneasily at the table, at the crumpled napkins and the drop of wine spilled by Luke's place, and shook her head. "I don't know what my mother would say, though."

"Come on," Theodora said. "They've left lights for us."

The fire in the little parlor was bright, and Theodora sat down beside the coffee tray while Luke brought brandy from the cupboard where he had carefully set it away the night before. "We must be cheerful at all costs," he said. "I'll challenge you again tonight, Doctor."

Before dinner they had ransacked the other downstairs rooms for comfortable chairs and lamps, and now their little parlor was easily the pleasantest room in the house. "Hill House has really been very kind to us," Theodora said, giving Eleanor her coffee, and Eleanor sat down gratefully in a pillowy, overstuffed chair. "No dirty dishes for Eleanor to wash, a pleasant evening in good company, and perhaps the sun shining again tomorrow."

"We must plan our picnic," Eleanor said.

"I am going to get fat and lazy in Hill House," Theodora went on. Her insistence on naming Hill House troubled Eleanor. It's as though she were saying it deliberately, Eleanor thought, telling the house she knows its name, calling the house to tell it where we are; is it bravado? "Hill House, Hill House, Hill House," Theodora said softly, and smiled across at Eleanor.

"Tell me," Luke said politely to Theodora, "since you *are* a princess, tell me about the political situation in your country."

"Very unsettled," Theodora said. "I ran away because my father, who is of course the king, insists that I marry Black Michael, who is the pretender to the throne. I, of course, cannot endure the sight of Black Michael, who wears one gold earring and beats his grooms with a riding crop."

"A most unstable country," Luke said. "How did you ever manage to get away?"

"I fled in a hay wagon, disguised as a milkmaid. They never thought to look for me there, and I crossed the border with papers I forged myself in a woodcutter's hut."

"And Black Michael will no doubt take over the country now in a *coup d'état?*"

"Undoubtedly. And he can have it."

It's like waiting in a dentist's office, Eleanor thought, watching them over her coffee cup; waiting in a dentist's office and listening to other patients make brave jokes across the room, all of you certain to meet the dentist sooner or later. She looked up suddenly, aware of the doctor near her, and smiled uncertainly.

"Nervous?" the doctor asked, and Eleanor nodded.

"Only because I wonder what's going to happen," she said.

"So do I." The doctor moved a chair and sat down beside her. "You have the feeling that something—whatever it is—is going to happen soon?"

"Yes. Everything seems to be waiting."

"And *they*"—the doctor nodded at Theodora and Luke, who were laughing at each other—"*they* meet it in *their* way; I wonder what it will do to all of us. I would have said a month ago that a situation like this would never really come about, that we four would sit here together, in this house." *He* does not name it, Eleanor noticed. "I've been waiting for a long time," he said.

"You think we are right to stay?"

"Right?" he said. "I think we are all incredibly silly to stay. I think that an atmosphere like this one can find out the flaws and faults and weaknesses in all of us, and break us apart in a matter of days. We have only one defense, and that is running away. At least it can't *follow* us, can it? When we feel ourselves endangered we can leave, just as we came. And," he added dryly, "just as fast as we can go."

"But we are forewarned," Eleanor said, "and there are four of us together."

"I have already mentioned this to Luke and Theodora," he said. "Promise me absolutely that you will leave, as fast as you can, if you begin to feel the house catching at you."

"I promise," Eleanor said, smiling. He is trying to make me feel braver, she thought, and was grateful. "It's all right, though," she told him. "Really, it's all right."

"I will feel no hesitation about sending you away," he said, rising, "if it seems to be necessary. Luke?" he said. "Will the ladies excuse us?"

While they set up the chessboard and men Theodora wandered, cup in hand, around the room, and Eleanor thought, She moves like an animal, nervous and alert; she can't sit still while there is any scent of disturbance in the air; we are all uneasy. "Come and sit by me," she said, and Theodora came, moving with grace, circling to a resting spot. She sat down in the chair the doctor had left, and leaned her head back tiredly; how lovely she is, Eleanor thought, how thoughtlessly, luckily lovely. "Are you tired?"

Theodora turned her head, smiling. "I can't stand waiting much longer."

"I was just thinking how relaxed you looked."

"And *I* was just thinking of—when was it? day before yesterday?—and wondering how I could have brought myself to leave there and come here. Possibly I'm homesick."

"Already?"

"Did you ever think about being homesick? If your home was Hill House would you be homesick for it? Did those two little girls cry for their dark, grim house when they were taken away?"

"I've never been away from anywhere," Eleanor said carefully, "so I suppose I've never been homesick."

"How about now? Your little apartment?"

"Perhaps," Eleanor said, looking into the fire, "I haven't had it long enough to believe it's my own."

"I want my own bed," Theodora said, and Eleanor

thought, She is sulking again; when she is hungry or tired or bored she turns into a baby. "I'm sleepy," Theodora said.

"It's after eleven," Eleanor said, and as she turned to glance at the chess game the doctor shouted with joyful triumph, and Luke laughed.

"Now, sir," the doctor said. "*Now*, sir."

"Fairly beaten, I admit," Luke said. He began to gather the chessmen and set them back into their box. "Any reason why I can't take a drop of brandy upstairs with me? To put myself to sleep, or give myself Dutch courage, or some such reason. Actually"—and he smiled over at Theodora and Eleanor—"I plan to stay up and read for a while."

"Are you still reading *Pamela*?" Eleanor asked the doctor.

"Volume two. I have three volumes to go, and then I shall begin *Clarissa Harlowe*, I think. Perhaps Luke would care to borrow—"

"No, thanks," Luke said hastily. "I have a suitcase full of mystery stories."

The doctor turned to look around. "Let me see," he said, "fire screened, lights out. Leave the doors for Mrs. Dudley to close in the morning."

Tiredly, following one another, they went up the great stairway, turning out lights behind them. "Has everyone got a flashlight, by the way?" the doctor asked, and they nodded, more intent upon sleep than the waves of darkness which came after them up the stairs of Hill House.

"Good night, everyone," Eleanor said, opening the door to the blue room.

"Good night," Luke said.

"Good night," Theodora said.

"Good night," the doctor said. "Sleep tight."

6

"Coming, mother, coming," Eleanor said, fumbling for the light. "It's all right, I'm coming." *Eleanor*, she heard, *Eleanor*. "Coming, coming," she shouted irritably, "just a *minute*, I'm *coming*."

"Eleanor?"

Then she thought, with a crashing shock which brought her awake, cold and shivering, out of bed and awake: *I am in Hill House*.

"What?" she cried out. "What? Theodora?"

"Eleanor? In here."

"Coming." No time for the light; she kicked a table out of the way, wondering at the noise of it, and struggled briefly with the door of the connecting bathroom. That is not the table falling, she thought; my mother is knocking on the wall. It was blessedly light in Theodora's room, and Theodora was sitting up in bed, her hair tangled from sleep and her eyes wide with the shock of awakening; I must look the same way, Eleanor thought, and said, "I'm here, what *is* it?"—and then heard, clearly for the first time, although she had been hearing it ever since she awakened. "What *is* it?" she whispered.

She sat down slowly on the foot of Theodora's bed, wondering at what seemed calmness in herself. Now, she thought, now. It is only a noise, and terribly cold, terribly, terribly cold. It is a noise down the hall, far down at the end, near the nursery door, and terribly cold, *not* my mother knocking on the wall.

"Something is knocking on the doors," Theodora said in a tone of pure rationality.

"That's all. And it's down near the other end of the hall. Luke and the doctor are probably there already, to see what is going on." Not at all like my mother knocking on the wall; I was dreaming again.

"Bang bang," Theodora said.

"Bang," Eleanor said, and giggled. I am calm, she thought, but so very cold; the noise is only a kind of banging on the doors, one after another; is this what I was so afraid about? "Bang" is the best word for it; it sounds like something children do, not mothers knocking against the wall for help, and anyway Luke and the doctor are there; is this what they mean by cold chills going up and down your back? Because it is not pleasant; it starts in your stomach and goes in waves around and up and down again like something alive. Like something alive. Yes. Like something alive.

"Theodora," she said, and closed her eyes and tightened her teeth together and wrapped her arms around herself, "it's getting closer."

"Just a noise," Theodora said, and moved next to Eleanor and sat tight against her. "It has an echo."

It sounded, Eleanor thought, like a hollow noise, a hollow bang, as though something were hitting the doors with an iron kettle, or an iron bar, or an iron glove. It pounded regularly for a minute, and then suddenly more softly, and then again in a quick flurry, seeming to be going methodically from door to door at the end of the hall. Distantly she thought she could hear the voices of Luke and the doctor, calling from somewhere below, and she thought, *Then they are not up here with us at all,* and heard the iron crashing against what must have been a door very close.

"Maybe it will go on down the other side of the hall," Theodora whispered, and Eleanor thought that the oddest part of this indescribable experience was that Theodora should be having it too. "No," Theodora said, and they heard the crash against the door across the hall. It was louder, it was deafening, it struck against the door next to them (did it move back and forth across the hall? did it go on feet along the carpet? did it lift a hand to the door?), and Eleanor threw herself away from the bed and ran to hold her hands against the door. "Go away," she shouted wildly. "Go away, go away!"

There was complete silence, and Eleanor thought, standing with her face against the door, Now I've done it; it was looking for the room with someone inside.

The cold crept and pinched at them, filling and overflowing the room. Anyone would have thought that the inhabitants of Hill House slept sweetly in this quiet, and then, so suddenly that Eleanor wheeled around, the sound of Theodora's teeth chattering, and Eleanor laughed. "You big baby," she said.

"I'm cold," Theodora said. "Deadly cold."

"So am I." Eleanor took the green quilt and threw it around Theodora, and took up Theodora's warm dressing gown and put it on. "You warmer now?"

"Where's Luke? Where's the doctor?"

"I don't know. Are you warmer now?"

"No." Theodora shivered.

"In a minute I'll go out in the hall and call them; are you—"

It started again, as though it had been listening, waiting to hear their voices and what they said, to identify them, to know how well prepared they were against it, waiting to hear if they were afraid. So suddenly that Eleanor leaped back against the bed and Theodora gasped and cried out, the iron crash came against their door, and both of them lifted their eyes in horror, because the hammering was against the upper edge of the door, higher than either of them could reach, higher than Luke or the doctor could reach, and the sickening, degrading cold came in waves from whatever was outside the door.

Eleanor stood perfectly still and looked at the door. She did not quite know what to do, although she believed that she was thinking coherently and was not unusually frightened, not more frightened, certainly, than she had believed in her worst dreams she could be. The cold troubled her even more than the sounds; even Theodora's warm robe was useless against the icy little curls of fingers on her back. The intelligent thing to do, perhaps, was to walk over and open the door; that, perhaps, would belong with the doctor's views of pure scientific inquiry. Eleanor knew that, even if her feet would take her as far as the door, her hand would not lift to the doorknob; impartially, remotely, she told herself that no one's hand would touch that knob; it's not the work hands were made for, she told herself. She had been rocking a little, each crash against the door pushing her a little backward, and now she was still because the noise was fading. "I'm going to complain to the janitor about the radiators," Theodora said from behind her. "Is it stopping?"

"No," Eleanor said, sick. "No."

It had found them. Since Eleanor would not open the door, it was going to make its own way in. Eleanor said aloud, "Now I know why people scream, because I think I'm going to," and Theodora said, "I will if you will," and laughed, so that Eleanor turned quickly back to the bed and they held each other, listening in silence. Little pattings came from around the doorframe, small seeking sounds, feeling the edges of the door, trying to sneak a way in. The doorknob was fondled, and Eleanor, whispering, asked, "Is it locked?" and Theodora nodded and then, wide-eyed, turned to stare at the connecting bathroom door. "Mine's locked too," Eleanor said against her ear, and Theodora closed her eyes in relief. The little sticky sounds moved on around the doorframe and then, as though a fury caught whatever was outside, the crashing came again, and Eleanor and Theodora saw the wood of the door tremble and shake, and the door move against its hinges.

"You can't get in," Eleanor said wildly, and again there was a silence, as though the house listened with attention to her words, understanding, cynically agreeing, content to wait. A thin little giggle came, in a breath of air through the room, a little mad rising laugh, the smallest whisper of a laugh, and Eleanor heard it all up and down her back, a little gloating laugh moving past them around the house, and then she heard the doctor and Luke calling from the stairs and, mercifully, it was over.

When the real silence came, Eleanor breathed shakily and moved stiffly. "We've been clutching each other like a couple of lost children," Theodora said and untwined her arms from around Eleanor's neck. "You're wearing my bathrobe."

"I forgot mine. Is it really over?"

"For tonight, anyway." Theodora spoke with certainty. "Can't you tell? Aren't you warm again?"

The sickening cold was gone, except for a reminiscent little thrill of it down Eleanor's back when she looked at the door. She began to pull at the tight knot she had put in the bathrobe cord, and said, "Intense cold is one of the symptoms of shock."

"Intense shock is one of the symptoms I've got," Theodora said. "Here come Luke and the doctor." Their voices were outside in the hall, speaking quickly, anxiously, and Eleanor dropped Theodora's robe on the bed and said, "For heaven's sake, don't let them knock on that door—one more knock would finish me"—and ran into her own room to get her own robe. Behind her she could hear Theodora telling them to wait a minute, and then going to unlock the door, and then Luke's voice saying pleasantly to Theodora, "Why, you look as though you'd seen a ghost."

When Eleanor came back she noticed that both Luke and the doctor were dressed, and it occurred to her that it might be a sound idea from now on; if that intense cold was going to come back at night it was going to find Eleanor sleeping in a wool suit and a heavy sweater, and she didn't care what Mrs. Dudley was going to say when she found that at least one of the lady guests was lying in one of the clean beds in heavy shoes and wool socks. "Well," she asked, "how do you gentlemen like living in a haunted house?"

"It's perfectly fine," Luke said, "perfectly fine. It gives me an excuse to have a drink in the middle of the night."

He had the brandy bottle and glasses, and Eleanor thought that they must make a companionable little group, the four of them, sitting around Theodora's room at four in the morning, drinking brandy. They spoke lightly, quickly, and gave one another fast, hidden, little curious glances, each of them wondering what secret terror had been tapped in the others, what changes might show in face or gesture, what unguarded weakness might have opened the way to ruin.

"Did anything happen in here while we were outside?" the doctor asked.

Eleanor and Theodora looked at each other and laughed, honestly at last, without any edge of hysteria or fear. After a minute Theodora said carefully, "Nothing in particular. Someone knocked on the door with a cannon ball and then tried to get in and eat us, and started laughing its head off when we wouldn't open the door. But nothing really out of the way."

Curiously, Eleanor went over and opened the door. "I thought the whole door was going to shatter," she said, bewildered, "and there isn't even a scratch on the wood, nor on any of the other doors; they're perfectly smooth."

"How nice that it didn't mar the woodwork," Theodora said, holding her brandy glass out to Luke. "I couldn't bear it if this dear old house got hurt." She grinned at Eleanor. "Nellie here was going to scream."

"So were you."

"Not at all; I only said so to keep you company. Besides, Mrs. Dudley already said she wouldn't come. And where were *you*, our manly defenders?"

"We were chasing a dog," Luke said. "At least, some animal like a dog." He stopped, and then went on reluctantly. "We followed it outside."

Theodora stared, and Eleanor said, "You mean it was *inside?*"

"I saw it run past my door," the doctor said, "just caught a glimpse of it, slipping along. I woke Luke and we followed it down the stairs and out into the garden and lost it somewhere back of the house."

"The front door was open?"

"No," Luke said. "The front door was closed. So were all the other doors. We checked."

"We've been wandering around for quite a while," the doctor said. "We never dreamed that you ladies were awake until we heard your voices." He spoke gravely. "There is one thing we have not taken into account," he said.

They looked at him, puzzled, and he explained, checking on his fingers in his lecture style. "First," he said, "Luke and I were awakened earlier than you ladies, clearly; we have been up and about, outside and in, for better than two hours, led on what you perhaps might allow me to call a wild-goose chase. Second, neither of us"—he glanced inquiringly at Luke as he spoke—"heard any sound up here until your voices began. It was perfectly quiet. That is, the sound which hammered on your door was not audible to us. When we gave up our vigil and decided to come upstairs we apparently drove away whatever was waiting outside your door. Now, as we sit here together, all is quiet."

"I still don't see what you mean," Theodora said, frowning.

"We must take precautions," he said.

"Against what? How?"

"When Luke and I are called outside, and you two are kept imprisoned inside, doesn't it begin to seem"—and his voice was very quiet—"doesn't it begin to seem that the intention is, somehow, to separate us?"

5

~~~~~~

LOOKING at herself in the mirror, with the bright morning sunlight freshening even the blue room of Hill House, Eleanor thought, It is my second morning in Hill House, and I am unbelievably happy. Journeys end in lovers meeting; I have spent an all but sleepless night, I have told lies and made a fool of myself, and the very air tastes like wine. I have been frightened half out of my foolish wits, but I have somehow earned this joy; I have been waiting for it for so long. Abandoning a lifelong belief that to name happiness is to dissipate it, she smiled at herself in the mirror and told herself silently, You are happy, Eleanor, you have finally been given a part of your measure of happiness. Looking away from her own face in the mirror, she thought blindly, Journeys end in lovers meeting, lovers meeting.

"Luke?" It was Theodora, calling outside in the hall. "You carried off one of my stockings last night, and you are a thieving cad, and I hope Mrs. Dudley can hear me."

Eleanor could hear Luke, faintly, answering; he protested that a gentleman had a right to keep the favors bestowed upon him by a lady, and he was absolutely certain that Mrs. Dudley could hear every word.

"Eleanor?" Now Theodora pounded on the connecting door. "Are you awake? May I come in?"

"Come, of course," Eleanor said, looking at her own face in the mirror. You deserve it, she told herself, you have spent your life earning it. Theodora opened the door and said happily, "How pretty you look this morning, my Nell. This curious life agrees with you."

Eleanor smiled at her; the life clearly agreed with Theodora too.

"We ought by rights to be walking around with dark circles under our eyes and a look of wild despair," Theodora said, putting an arm around Eleanor and looking into the mirror beside her, "and look at us—two blooming, fresh young lovelies."

"I'm thirty-four years old," Eleanor said, and wondered what obscure defiance made her add two years.

"And you look about fourteen," Theodora said. "Come along; we've earned our breakfast."

Laughing, they raced down the great staircase and found

their way through the game room and into the dining room. "Good morning," Luke said brightly. "And how did everyone sleep?"

"Delightfully, thank you," Eleanor said. "Like a baby."

"There may have been a little noise," Theodora said, "but one has to expect that in these old houses. Doctor, what do we do this morning?"

"Hm?" said the doctor, looking up. He alone looked tired, but his eyes were lighted with the same brightness they found, all, in one another; it is excitement, Eleanor thought; we are all enjoying ourselves.

"Ballechin House," the doctor said, savoring his words. "Borley Rectory. Glamis Castle. It is incredible to find oneself experiencing it, absolutely incredible. I could *not* have believed it. I begin to understand, dimly, the remote delight of your true medium. I think I shall have the marmalade, if you would be so kind. Thank you. My wife will never believe me. Food has a new flavor—do you find it so?"

"It isn't just that Mrs. Dudley has surpassed herself, then; I was wondering," Luke said.

"I've been trying to remember," Eleanor said. "About last night, I mean. I can remember *knowing* that I was frightened, but I can't imagine actually *being* frightened—"

"I remember the cold," Theodora said, and shivered.

"I think it's because it was so unreal by any pattern of thought I'm used to; I mean, it just didn't make *sense*." Eleanor stopped and laughed, embarrassed.

"I agree," Luke said. "I found myself this morning *telling* myself what had happened last night; the reverse of a bad dream, as a matter of fact, where you keep telling yourself that it *didn't* really happen."

"I thought it was exciting," Theodora said.

The doctor lifted a warning finger. "It is still perfectly possible that it is all caused by subterranean waters."

"Then more houses ought to be built over secret springs," Theodora said.

The doctor frowned. "This excitement troubles me," he said. "It is intoxicating, certainly, but might it not also be dangerous? An effect of the atmosphere of Hill House? The first sign that we have—as it were—fallen under a spell?"

"Then I will be an enchanted princess," Theodora said.

"And yet," Luke said, "if last night is a true measure of Hill House, we are not going to have much trouble; we were frightened, certainly, and found the experience unpleasant while it was going on, and yet I cannot remember that I felt in any *physical* danger; even Theodora telling that whatever was outside her door was coming to eat her did not really sound—"

"I know what she meant," Eleanor said, "because I thought it was exactly the right word. The sense was that it wanted to consume us, take us into itself, make us a part of the house, maybe—oh, dear. I thought I knew what I was saying, but I'm doing it very badly."

"No physical danger exists," the doctor said positively. "No ghost in all the long histories of ghosts has ever hurt anyone physically. The only damage done is by the victim to himself. One cannot even say that the ghost attacks the mind, because the mind, the conscious, thinking mind, is invulnerable; in all our conscious minds, as we sit here talking, there is not one iota of belief in ghosts. Not one of us, even after last night, can say the word 'ghost' without a little involuntary smile. No, the menace of the supernatural is that it attacks where modern minds are weakest, where we have abandoned our protective armor of superstition and have no substitute defense. Not one of us thinks rationally that what ran through the garden last night was a ghost, and what knocked on the door was a ghost, and yet there was certainly *something* going on in Hill House last night, and the mind's instinctive refuge—self-doubt—is eliminated. We cannot say, 'It was my imagination,' because three other people were there too."

"I could say," Eleanor put in, smiling, " 'All three of you are in my imagination; none of this is real.' "

"If I thought you could really believe that," the doctor said gravely, "I would turn you out of Hill House this morning. You would be venturing far too close to the state of mind which would welcome the perils of Hill House with a kind of sisterly embrace."

"He means he would think you were batty, Nell dear."

"Well," Eleanor said, "I expect I would be. If I had to take sides with Hill House against the rest of you, I would expect you to send me away." Why me, she wondered, why me? Am I the public conscience? Expected always to say in cold words what the rest of them are too arrogant to recognize? Am I supposed to be the weakest, weaker than Theodora? Of all of us, she thought, I am surely the one least likely to turn against the others.

"Poltergeists are another thing altogether," the doctor said, his eyes resting briefly on Eleanor. "They deal entirely with the physical world; they throw stones, they move objects, they smash dishes; Mrs. Foyster at Borley Rectory was a long-suffering woman, but she finally lost her temper entirely when her best teapot was hurled through the window. Poltergeists, however, are rock-bottom on the supernatural social scale; they are destructive, but mindless and will-less; they are merely undirected force. Do you recall," he asked with a little smile, "Oscar Wilde's lovely story, 'The Canterville Ghost'?"

"The American twins who routed the fine old English ghost," Theodora said.

"Exactly. I have always liked the notion that the American twins were actually a poltergeist phenomenon; certainly poltergeists can overshadow any more interesting manifestation. Bad ghosts drive out good." And he patted his hands happily. "They drive out everything else, too," he added. "There is a manor in Scotland, infested with poltergeists, where as many as seventeen spontaneous fires have broken out in one day; poltergeists like to turn people out of bed violently by tipping the bed end over end, and I remember the case of a minister who was forced to leave his home because he was tormented, day after day, by a poltergeist who hurled at his head hymn books stolen from a rival church."

Suddenly, without reason, laughter trembled inside Eleanor; she wanted to run to the head of the table and hug the doctor, she wanted to reel, chanting, across the stretches of the lawn, she wanted to sing and to shout and to fling her arms and move in great emphatic, possessing circles around the rooms of Hill House; I am here, I am here, she thought. She shut her eyes quickly in delight and then said demurely to the doctor, "And what do we do today?"

"You're still like a pack of children," the doctor said, smiling too. "Always asking me what to do today. Can't you amuse yourselves with your toys? Or with each other? *I* have work to do."

"All I *really* want to do"—and Theodora giggled—"is slide down that banister." The excited gaiety had caught her as it had Eleanor.

"Hide and seek," Luke said.

"Try not to wander around alone too much," the doctor said. "I can't think of a good reason why not, but it does seem sensible."

"Because there are bears in the woods," Theodora said.

"And tigers in the attic," Eleanor said.

"And an old witch in the tower, and a dragon in the drawing room."

"I am quite serious," the doctor said, laughing.

"It's ten o'clock. I clear—"

"Good morning, Mrs. Dudley," the doctor said, and Eleanor and Theodora and Luke leaned back and laughed helplessly.

"I clear at ten o'clock."

"We won't keep you long. About fifteen minutes, please, and then you can clear the table."

"I clear breakfast at ten o'clock. I set on lunch at one. Dinner I set on at six. It's ten o'clock."

"Mrs. Dudley," the doctor began sternly, and then, noticing Luke's face tight with silent laughter, lifted his napkin to cover his eyes, and gave in. "You may clear the table, Mrs. Dudley," the doctor said brokenly.

Happily, the sound of their laughter echoing along the halls of Hill House and carrying to the marble group in the drawing room and the nursery upstairs and the odd little top to the tower, they made their way down the passage to their parlor and fell, still laughing, into chairs. "We must not make fun of Mrs. Dudley," the doctor said and leaned forward, his face in his hands and his shoulders shaking.

They laughed for a long time, speaking now and then in half-phrases, trying to tell one another something, pointing at one another wildly, and their laughter rocked Hill House until, weak and aching, they lay back, spent, and regarded one another. "Now—" the doctor began, and was stopped by a little giggling burst from Theodora.

"Now," the doctor said again, more severely, and they were quiet. "I want more coffee," he said, appealing. "Don't we all?"

"You mean go right in there and ask Mrs. Dudley?" Eleanor asked.

"Walk right up to her when it isn't one o'clock or six o'clock and just *ask* her for some coffee?" Theodora demanded.

"Roughly, yes," the doctor said. "Luke, my boy, I have observed that you are already something of a favorite with Mrs. Dudley—"

"And how," Luke inquired with amazement, "did you ever manage to observe anything so unlikely? Mrs. Dudley regards me with the same particular loathing she gives a dish not properly on its shelf; in Mrs. Dudley's eyes—"

"You are, after all, the heir to the house," the doctor

said coaxingly. "Mrs. Dudley must feel for you as an old family retainer feels for the young master."

"In Mrs. Dudley's eyes I am something lower than a dropped fork. I beg of you, if you are contemplating asking the old fool for something, send Theo, or our charming Nell. *They* are not afraid—"

"Nope," Theodora said. "You can't send a helpless female to face down Mrs. Dudley. Nell and I are here to be protected, not to man the battlements for you cowards."

"The doctor—"

"Nonsense," the doctor said heartily. "You certainly wouldn't think of asking *me*, an older man; anyway, you *know* she adores you."

"Insolent graybeard," Luke said. "Sacrificing me for a cup of coffee. Do not be surprised, and I say it darkly, do not be surprised if you lose your Luke in this cause; perhaps Mrs. Dudley has not yet had her own midmorning snack, and she is perfectly capable of a *filet de Luke à la meunière*, or perhaps *dieppoise*, depending upon her mood; if I do not return"—and he shook his finger warningly under the doctor's nose—"I entreat you to regard your lunch with the gravest suspicion." Bowing extravagantly, as befitted one off to slay a giant, he closed the door behind him.

"Lovely Luke." Theodora stretched luxuriously.

"Lovely Hill House," Eleanor said. "Theo, there is a kind of little summerhouse in the side garden, all overgrown; I noticed it yesterday. Can we explore it this morning?"

"Delighted," Theodora said. "I would not like to leave one inch of Hill House uncherished. Anyway, it's too nice a day to stay inside."

"We'll ask Luke to come too," Eleanor said. "And you, Doctor?"

"My notes—" the doctor began, and then stopped as the door opened so suddenly that in Eleanor's mind was only the thought that Luke had not dared face Mrs. Dudley after all, but had stood, waiting, pressed against the door; then, looking at his white face and hearing the doctor say with fury, "I broke my own first rule; I sent him alone," she found herself only asking urgently, "Luke? Luke?"

"It's all right." Luke even smiled. "But come into the long hallway."

Chilled by his face and his voice and his smile, they got up silently and followed him through the doorway into the dark long hallway which led back to the front hall. "Here," Luke said, and a little winding shiver of sickness went down Eleanor's back when she saw that he was holding a lighted match up to the wall.

"It's—writing?" Eleanor asked, pressing closer to see.

"Writing," Luke said. "I didn't even notice it until I was coming back. Mrs. Dudley said no," he added, his voice tight.

"My flash." The doctor took his flashlight from his pocket, and under its light, as he moved slowly from one end of the hall to the other, the letters stood out clearly. "Chalk," the doctor said, stepping forward to touch a letter with the tip of his finger. "Written in chalk."

The writing was large and straggling and ought to have looked, Eleanor thought, as though it had been scribbled by bad boys on a fence. Instead, it was incredibly real, going in broken lines over the thick paneling of the hallway. From one end of the hallway to the other the letters went, almost too large to read, even when she stood back against the opposite wall.

"Can you read it?" Luke asked softly, and the doctor, moving his flashlight, read slowly: HELP ELEANOR COME HOME.

"No." And Eleanor felt the words stop in her throat; she had seen her name as the doctor read it. It is me, she thought. It is my name standing out there so clearly; I should not be on the walls of this house. "Wipe it off, *please*," she said, and felt Theodora's arm go around her shoulders. "It's *crazy*," Eleanor said, bewildered.

"Crazy is the word, all right," Theodora said strongly. "Come back inside, Nell, and sit down. Luke will get something and wipe it off."

"But it's *crazy*," Eleanor said, hanging back to see her name on the wall. "*Why—?*"

Firmly the doctor put her through the door into the little parlor and closed it; Luke had already attacked the message with his handkerchief. "Now you listen to me," the doctor said to Eleanor. "Just because your name—"

"That's it," Eleanor said, staring at him. "It knows my name, doesn't it? It knows *my* name."

"Shut up, will you?" Theodora shook her violently. "It could have said any of us; it knows *all* our names."

"Did you write it?" Eleanor turned to Theodora. "Please tell me—I won't be angry or anything, just so I can know that—maybe it was only a joke? To frighten me?" She looked appealingly at the doctor.

"You know that none of us wrote it," the doctor said.

Luke came in, wiping his hands on his handkerchief, and

Eleanor turned hopefully. "Luke," she said, "you wrote it, didn't you? When you went out?"

Luke stared, and then came to sit on the arm of her chair. "Listen," he said, "you want me to go writing your name everywhere? Carving your initials on trees? Writing 'Eleanor, Eleanor' on little scraps of paper?" He gave her hair a soft little pull. "I've got more sense," he said. "Behave yourself."

"Then why me?" Eleanor said, looking from one of them to another; I am outside, she thought madly, I am the one chosen, and she said quickly, beggingly, "Did I do something to attract attention, more than anyone else?"

"No more than usual, dear," Theodora said. She was standing by the fireplace, leaning on the mantel and tapping her fingers, and when she spoke she looked at Eleanor with a bright smile. "Maybe you wrote it yourself."

Angry, Eleanor almost shouted. "You think I *want* to see my name scribbled all over this foul house? You think *I* like the idea that I'm the center of attention? *I'm* not the spoiled baby, after all—*I* don't like being singled out—"

"Asking for help, did you notice?" Theodora said lightly. "Perhaps the spirit of the poor little companion has found a means of communication at last. Maybe she was only waiting for some drab, timid—"

"Maybe it was only addressed to me because no possible appeal for help could get through that iron selfishness of yours; maybe I might have more sympathy and understanding in one minute than—"

"And maybe, of course, you wrote it to yourself," Theodora said again.

After the manner of men who see women quarreling, the doctor and Luke had withdrawn, standing tight together in miserable silence; now, at last, Luke moved and spoke. "That's enough, Eleanor," he said, unbelievably, and Eleanor whirled around, stamping. "How dare you?" she said, gasping. "How *dare* you?"

And the doctor laughed, then, and she stared at him and then at Luke, who was smiling and watching her. What is wrong with me? she thought. Then—but they think Theodora did it on purpose, made me mad so I wouldn't be frightened; how shameful to be maneuvered that way. She covered her face and sat down in her chair.

"Nell, dear," Theodora said, "I *am* sorry."

I must say something, Eleanor told herself; I must show them that I am a good sport, after all; a good sport; let them think that I am ashamed of myself. "*I*'m sorry," she said. "I was frightened."

"Of course you were," the doctor said, and Eleanor thought, How simple he is, how transparent; he believes every silly thing he has ever heard. He thinks, even, that Theodora shocked me out of hysteria. She smiled at him and thought, Now I am back in the fold.

"I really thought you were going to start shrieking," Theodora said, coming to kneel by Eleanor's chair. "*I* would have, in your place. But we can't afford to have you break up, you know."

We can't afford to have anyone but Theodora in the center of the stage, Eleanor thought; if Eleanor is going to be the outsider, she is going to be it all alone. She reached out and patted Theodora's head and said, "Thanks. I guess I was kind of shaky for a minute."

"I wondered if you two were going to come to blows," Luke said, "until I realized what Theodora was doing."

Smiling down into Theodora's bright, happy eyes, Eleanor thought, But that isn't what Theodora was doing at all.

2

Time passed lazily at Hill House. Eleanor and Theodora, the doctor and Luke, alert against terror, wrapped around by the rich hills and securely set into the warm, dark luxuries of the house, were permitted a quiet day and a quiet night—enough, perhaps, to dull them a little. They took their meals together, and Mrs. Dudley's cooking stayed perfect. They talked together and played chess; the doctor finished *Pamela* and began on *Sir Charles Grandison*. A compelling need for occasional privacy led them to spend some hours alone in their separate rooms, without disturbance. Theodora and Eleanor and Luke explored the tangled thicket behind the house and found the little summerhouse, while the doctor sat on the wide lawn, writing, within sight and hearing. They found a walled-in rose garden, grown over with weeds, and a vegetable garden tenderly nourished by the Dudleys. They spoke often of arranging their picnic by the brook. There were wild strawberries near the summerhouse, and Theodora and Eleanor and Luke brought back a handkerchief full and lay on the lawn near the doctor, eating them, staining their hands and their mouths; like children, the doctor told them, looking up with amusement from his notes. Each of them had written—carelessly, and with little attention to detail—an account of what they thought they had seen and heard so far in Hill House, and the doctor had put the papers away in his portfolio. The next morning—their third morning in Hill House—the doctor, aided by Luke, had spent a loving and maddening hour on the floor of the upstairs hall, trying, with chalk and measuring tape, to determine the precise dimensions of the cold spot, while Eleanor and Theodora sat cross-legged on the hall floor, noting down the doctor's measurements and playing tic-tac-toe. The doctor was considerably hampered in his work by the fact that, his hands repeatedly chilled by the extreme cold, he could not hold either the chalk or the tape for more than a minute at a time. Luke, inside the nursery doorway, could hold one end of the tape until his hand came into the cold spot, and then his fingers lost strength and relaxed helplessly. A thermometer, dropped into the center of the cold spot, refused to register any change at all, but continued doggedly maintaining that the temperature there was the same as the temperature down the rest of the hall, causing the doctor to fume wildly against the statisticians of Borley Rectory, who had caught an eleven-degree drop. When he had defined the cold spot as well as he could, and noted his results in his notebook, he brought them downstairs for lunch and issued a general challenge to them, to meet him at croquet in the cool of the afternoon.

"It seems foolish," he explained, "to spend a morning as glorious as this has been looking at a frigid place on a floor. We must plan to spend more time outside"—and was mildly surprised when they laughed.

"Is there still a world somewhere?" Eleanor asked wonderingly. Mrs. Dudley had made them a peach shortcake, and she looked down at her plate and said, "I am sure Mrs.

Dudley goes somewhere else at night, and she brings back heavy cream each morning, and Dudley comes up with groceries every afternoon, but as far as I can remember there is no other place than this."

"We are on a desert island," Luke said.

"I can't picture any world but Hill House," Eleanor said.

"Perhaps," Theodora said, "we should make notches on a stick, or pile pebbles in a heap, one each day, so we will know how long we have been marooned."

"How pleasant not to have any word from outside." Luke helped himself to an enormous heap of whipped cream. "No letters, no newspapers; anything might be happening."

"Unfortunately—" the doctor said, and then stopped. "I beg your pardon," he went on. "I meant only to say that word *will* be reaching us from outside, and of course it is not unfortunate at all. Mrs. Montague—my wife, that is—will be here on Saturday."

"But when is Saturday?" Luke asked. "Delighted to see Mrs. Montague, of course."

"Day after tomorrow." The doctor thought. "Yes," he said after a minute, "I believe that the day after tomorrow is Saturday. We will know it is Saturday, of course," he told them with a little twinkle, "because Mrs. Montague will be here."

"I hope she is not holding high hopes of things going bump in the night," Theodora said. "Hill House has fallen far short of its original promise, I think. Or perhaps Mrs. Montague will be greeted with a volley of psychic experiences."

"Mrs. Montague," the doctor said, "will be perfectly ready to receive them."

"I wonder," Theodora said to Eleanor as they left the lunch table under Mrs. Dudley's watchful eye, "why everything *has* been so quiet. I think this waiting is nerve-racking, almost worse than having something happen."

"It's not us doing the waiting," Eleanor said. "It's the house. I think it's biding its time."

"Waiting until we feel secure, maybe, and then it will pounce."

"I wonder how long it can wait." Eleanor shivered and started up the great staircase. "I am almost tempted to write a letter to my sister. You know—'Having a perfectly *splendid* time here in jolly old Hill House. . . .'"

" 'You really must plan to bring the whole family next summer,' " Theodora went on. " 'We sleep under blankets every night. . . .' "

" 'The air is so bracing, particularly in the upstairs hall. . . .' "

" 'You go around all the time just glad to be alive. . . .' "

" 'There's something going on every minute. . . .' "

" 'Civilization seems so far away. . . .' "

Eleanor laughed. She was ahead of Theodora, at the top of the stairs. The dark hallway was a little lightened this afternoon, because they had left the nursery door open and the sunlight came through the windows by the tower and touched the doctor's measuring tape and chalk on the floor. The light reflected from the stained-glass window on the stair landing and made shattered fragments of blue and orange and green on the dark wood of the hall. "I'm going to sleep," she said. "I've never been so lazy in my life."

"I'm going to lie on my bed and dream about streetcars," Theodora said.

It had become Eleanor's habit to hesitate in the doorway of her room, glancing around quickly before she went inside; she told herself that this was because the room was so exceedingly blue and always took a moment to get used to. When she came inside she went across to open the window, which she always found closed; today she was half-way across the room before she heard Theodora's door slam back, and Theodora's smothered "Eleanor!" Moving quickly, Eleanor ran into the hall and to Theodora's doorway, to stop, aghast, looking over Theodora's shoulder. "What *is* it?" she whispered.

"What does it *look* like?" Theodora's voice rose crazily. "What does it *look* like, you fool?"

And I won't forgive her *that*, either, Eleanor thought concretely through her bewilderment. "It looks like paint," she said hesitantly. "Except"—realizing—"except the smell is awful."

"It's blood," Theodora said with finality. She clung to the door, swaying as the door moved, staring. "Blood," she said. "All over. Do you see it?"

"Of course I see it. And it's not *all* over. Stop making such a fuss." Although, she thought conscientiously, Theodora was making very little of a fuss, actually. One of these times, she thought, one of us *is* going to put her head back and really howl, and I hope it won't be me, because I'm trying to guard against it; it *will* be Theodora who . . . And then, cold, she asked, "Is that more writing on the wall?"—and heard Theodora's wild laugh, and thought, Maybe it will be me, after all, and I can't afford to. I must be steady, and she closed her eyes and found herself saying silently, O stay and hear, your true love's coming, that can sing both high and low. Trip no further, pretty sweeting; journeys end in lovers meeting . . .

"Yes indeed, dear," Theodora said. "I don't know how you managed it."

Every wise man's son doth know. "Be sensible," Eleanor said. "Call Luke. And the doctor."

"Why?" Theodora asked. "Wasn't it to be just a little private surprise for me? A secret just for the two of us?" Then, pulling away from Eleanor, who tried to hold her from going farther into the room, she ran to the great wardrobe and threw open the door and, cruelly, began to cry. "My clothes," she said. "My clothes."

Steadily Eleanor turned and went to the top of the stairs. "Luke," she called, leaning over the banisters. "Doctor." Her voice was not loud, and she had tried to keep it level, but she heard the doctor's book drop to the floor and then the pounding of feet as he and Luke ran for the stairs. She watched them, seeing their apprehensive faces, wondering at the uneasiness which lay so close below the surface in all of them, so that each of them seemed always waiting for a cry for help from one of the others; intelligence and understanding are really no protection at all, she thought. "It's Theo," she said as they came to the top of the stairs. "She's hysterical. Someone—something—has gotten red paint in her room, and she's crying over her clothes." Now I could not have put it more fairly than that, she thought, turning to follow them. Could I have put it more fairly than that? she asked herself, and found that she was smiling.

Theodora was still sobbing wildly in her room and kicking at the wardrobe door, in a tantrum that might have been laughable if she had not been holding her yellow shirt, matted and stained; her other clothes had been torn from the hangers and lay trampled and disordered on the wardrobe floor, all of them smeared and reddened. "What is it?" Luke asked the doctor, and the doctor, shaking his head, said, "I would swear that it was blood, and yet to get so much blood one would almost have to . . ." and then was abruptly quiet.

All of them stood in silence for a moment and looked at HELP ELEANOR COME HOME ELEANOR written in shaky red letters on the wallpaper over Theodora's bed.

This time I am ready, Eleanor told herself, and said, "You'd better get her out of here; bring her into my room."

"My clothes are ruined," Theodora said to the doctor. "Do you see my clothes?"

The smell was atrocious, and the writing on the wall had dripped and splattered. There was a line of drops from the wall to the wardrobe—perhaps what had first turned Theodora's attention that way—and a great irregular stain on the green rug. "It's disgusting," Eleanor said. "Please get Theo into my room."

Luke and the doctor between them persuaded Theodora through the bathroom and into Eleanor's room, and Eleanor, looking at the red paint (It must be paint, she told herself; it's simply *got* to be paint; what else *could* it be?), said aloud, "But *why?*"—and stared up at the writing on the wall. Here lies one, she thought gracefully, whose name was writ in blood; is it possible that I am not quite coherent at this moment?

"Is she all right?" she asked, turning as the doctor came back into the room.

"She will be in a few minutes. We'll have to move her in with you for a while, I should think; I can't imagine her wanting to sleep in *here* again." The doctor smiled a little wanly. "It will be a long time, I think, before she opens another door by herself."

"I suppose she'll have to wear my clothes."

"I suppose she will, if you don't mind." The doctor looked at her curiously. "This message troubles you less than the other?"

"It's too silly," Eleanor said, trying to understand her own feelings. "I've been standing here looking at it and just wondering *why*. I mean, it's like a joke that didn't come off; I was supposed to be *much* more frightened than this, I think, and I'm not because it's simply *too* horrible to be real. And I keep remembering Theo putting red polish . . ." She giggled, and the doctor looked at her sharply, but she went on, "It might as *well* be paint, don't you see?" I can't stop talking, she thought; what do *I* have to explain in all this? "Maybe I can't take it seriously," she said, "after the sight of Theo screaming over her poor clothes and accusing me of writing my name all over her wall. Maybe I'm getting used to her blaming me for everything."

"Nobody's blaming you for anything," the doctor said, and Eleanor felt that she had been reproved.

"I hope my clothes will be good enough for her," she said tartly.

The doctor turned, looking around the room; he touched one finger gingerly to the letters on the wall and moved

Theodora's yellow shirt with his foot. "Later," he said absently. "Tomorrow, perhaps." He glanced at Eleanor and smiled. "I can make an exact sketch of this," he said.

"I can help you," Eleanor said. "It makes me sick, but it doesn't frighten me."

"Yes," the doctor said. "I think we'd better close up the room for now, however; we don't want Theodora blundering in here again. Then later, at my leisure, I can study it. Also," he said with a flash of amusement, "I would not like to have Mrs. Dudley coming in here to straighten up."

Eleanor watched silently while he locked the hall door from inside the room, and then they went through the bathroom and he locked the connecting door into Theodora's green room. "I'll see about moving in another bed," he said, and then, with some awkwardness, "You've kept your head well, Eleanor; it's a help to me."

"I told you, it makes me sick but it doesn't frighten me," she said, pleased, and turned to Theodora. Theodora was lying on Eleanor's bed, and Eleanor saw with a queasy turn that Theodora had gotten red on her hands and it was rubbing off onto Eleanor's pillow. "Look," she said harshly, coming over to Theodora, "you'll have to wear my clothes until you get new ones, or until we get the others cleaned."

"Cleaned?" Theodora rolled convulsively on the bed and pressed her stained hands against her eyes. "*Cleaned?*"

"For heaven's sake," Eleanor said, "let me wash you off." She thought, without trying to find a reason, that she had never felt such uncontrollable loathing for any person before, and she went into the bathroom and soaked a towel and came back to scrub roughly at Theodora's hands and face. "You're filthy with the stuff," she said, hating to touch Theodora.

Suddenly Theodora smiled at her. "I don't really think you did it," she said, and Eleanor turned to see that Luke was behind her, looking down at them. "What a fool I am," Theodora said to him, and Luke laughed.

"You will be a delight in Nell's red sweater," he said.

She is wicked, Eleanor thought, beastly and soiled and dirty. She took the towel into the bathroom and left it to soak in cold water; when she came out Luke was saying, ". . . another bed in here; you girls are going to share a room from now on."

"Share a room and share our clothes," Theodora said. "We're going to be practically twins."

"Cousins," Eleanor said, but no one heard her.

3

"It was the custom, rigidly adhered to," Luke said, turning the brandy in his glass, "for the public executioner, before a quartering, to outline his knife strokes in chalk upon the belly of his victim—for fear of a slip, you understand."

I would like to hit her with a stick, Eleanor thought, looking down on Theodora's head beside her chair; I would like to batter her with rocks.

"An exquisite refinement, exquisite. Because of course the chalk strokes would have been almost unbearable, excruciating, if the victim were ticklish."

I hate her, Eleanor thought, she sickens me; she is all washed and clean and wearing my red sweater.

"When the death was by hanging in chains, however, the executioner . . ."

"Nell?" Theodora looked up at her and smiled. "I really am sorry, you know," she said.

I would like to watch her dying, Eleanor thought, and smiled back and said, "Don't be silly."

"Among the Sufis there is a teaching that the universe has never been created and consequently cannot be destroyed. I have spent the afternoon," Luke announced gravely, "browsing in our little library."

The doctor sighed. "No chess tonight, I think," he said to Luke, and Luke nodded. "It has been an exhausting day," the doctor said, "and I think you ladies should retire early."

"Not until I am well dulled with brandy," Theodora said firmly.

"Fear," the doctor said, "is the relinquishment of logic, the *willing* relinquishing of reasonable patterns. We yield to it or we fight it, but we cannot meet it halfway."

"I was wondering earlier," Eleanor said, feeling she had somehow an apology to make to all of them. "I thought I was altogether calm, and yet now I know I was terribly afraid." She frowned, puzzled, and they waited for her to go on. "When I *am* afraid, I can see perfectly the sensible, beautiful not-afraid side of the world, I can see chairs and tables and windows staying the same, not affected in the least, and I can see things like the careful woven texture of the carpet, not even moving. But when I am afraid I no longer exist in any relation to these things. I suppose because things are *not* afraid."

"I think we are only afraid of ourselves," the doctor said slowly.

"No," Luke said. "Of seeing ourselves clearly and without disguise."

"Of knowing what we really want," Theodora said. She pressed her cheek against Eleanor's hand and Eleanor, hating the touch of her, took her hand away quickly.

"I am always afraid of being alone," Eleanor said, and wondered, Am *I* talking like this? Am I saying something I will regret bitterly tomorrow? Am I making more guilt for myself? "Those letters spelled out *my* name, and none of you know what that feels like—it's so *familiar*." And she gestured to them, almost in appeal. "Try to *see*," she said. "It's my own dear name, and it belongs to me, and something is using it and writing it and calling me with it and my own *name* . . ." She stopped and said, looking from one of them to another, even down onto Theodora's face looking up at her, "Look. There's only one of me, and it's all I've got. I *hate* seeing myself dissolve and slip and separate so that I'm living in one half, my mind, and I see the other half of me helpless and frantic and driven and I can't stop it, but I know I'm not really going to be hurt and yet time is so long and even a second goes on and on and I could stand any of it if I could only surrender—"

"*Surrender?*" said the doctor sharply, and Eleanor stared.

"Surrender?" Luke repeated.

"I don't know," Eleanor said, perplexed. I was just talking along, she told herself, I was saying something—what was I just saying?

"She has done this before," Luke said to the doctor.

"I know," said the doctor gravely, and Eleanor could feel them all looking at her. "I'm sorry," she said. "Did I make a fool of myself? It's probably because I'm tired."

"Not at all," the doctor said, still grave. "Drink your brandy."

"Brandy?" And Eleanor looked down, realizing that she held a brandy glass. "What did I *say?*" she asked them.

Theodora chuckled. "Drink," she said. "You need it, my Nell."

Obediently Eleanor sipped at her brandy, feeling clearly its sharp burn, and then said to the doctor, "I must have said something silly, from the way you're all staring at me."

The doctor laughed. "Stop trying to be the center of attention."

"Vanity," Luke said serenely.

"Have to be in the limelight," Theodora said, and they smiled fondly, all looking at Eleanor.

4

Sitting up in the two beds beside each other, Eleanor and Theodora reached out between and held hands tight; the room was brutally cold and thickly dark. From the room next door, the room which until that morning had been Theodora's, came the steady low sound of a voice babbling, too low for words to be understood, too steady for disbelief. Holding hands so hard that each of them could feel the other's bones, Eleanor and Theodora listened, and the low, steady sound went on and on, the voice lifting sometimes for an emphasis on a mumbled word, falling sometimes to a breath, going on and on. Then, without warning, there was a little laugh, the small gurgling laugh that broke through the babbling, and rose as it laughed, on up and up the scale, and then broke off suddenly in a little painful gasp, and the voice went on.

Theodora's grasp loosened, and tightened, and Eleanor,

lulled for a minute by the sounds, started and looked across to where Theodora ought to be in the darkness, and then thought, screamingly, Why is it dark? *Why is it dark?* She rolled and clutched Theodora's hand with both of hers, and tried to speak and could not, and held on, blindly, and frozen, trying to stand her mind on its feet, trying to reason again. We left the light on, she told herself, so why is it dark? Theodora, she tried to whisper, and her mouth could not move; Theodora, she tried to ask, why is it dark? and the voice went on, babbling, low and steady, a little liquid gloating sound. She thought she might be able to distinguish words if she lay perfectly still, if she lay perfectly still, and listened, and listened and heard the voice going on and on, never ceasing, and she hung desperately to Theodora's hand and felt an answering weight on her own hand.

Then the little gurgling laugh came again, and the rising mad sound of it drowned out the voice, and then suddenly absolute silence. Eleanor took a breath, wondering if she could speak now, and then she heard a little soft cry which broke her heart, a little infinitely sad cry, a little sweet moan of wild sadness. It is a *child*, she thought with disbelief, a child is crying somewhere, and then, upon that thought, came the wild shrieking voice she had never heard before and yet knew she had heard always in her nightmares. "Go away!" it screamed. "Go away, go away, don't hurt me," and, after, sobbing, "Please don't hurt me. Please let me go home," and then the little sad crying again.

I can't stand it, Eleanor thought concretely. This is monstrous, this is cruel, they have been hurting a child and I won't let anyone hurt a child, and the babbling went on, low and steady, on and on and on, the voice rising a little and falling a little, going on and on.

Now, Eleanor thought, perceiving that she was lying sideways on the bed in the black darkness, holding with both hands to Theodora's hand, holding so tight she could feel the fine bones of Theodora's fingers, now, I will not endure this. They think to scare me. Well, they have. I am scared, but more than that, I am a person, I am human, I am a walking reasoning humorous human being and I will take a lot from this lunatic filthy house but I will not go along with hurting a child, no, I will not; I will by God get my mouth to open right now and I will yell I will I will yell "STOP IT," she shouted, and the lights were on the way they had left them and Theodora was sitting up in bed, startled and disheveled.

"What?" Theodora was saying. "What, Nell? What?"

"God God," Eleanor said, flinging herself out of bed and across the room to stand shuddering in a corner, "God God—whose hand was I holding?"

6

―――――――――

I A M learning the pathways of the heart, Eleanor thought quite seriously, and then wondered what she could have meant by thinking any such thing. It was afternoon, and she sat in the sunlight on the steps of the summerhouse beside Luke; these are the silent pathways of the heart, she thought. She knew that she was pale, and still shaken, with dark circles under her eyes, but the sun was warm and the leaves moved gently overhead, and Luke beside her lay lazily against the step. "Luke," she asked, going slowly for fear of ridicule, "why do people want to talk to each other?

I mean, what are the things people always want to find out about other people?"

"What do you want to know about me, for instance?" He laughed. She thought, But why not ask what *he* wants to know about *me;* he is so extremely vain—and laughed in turn and said, "What can I *ever* know about you, beyond what I see?" *See* was the least of the words she might have chosen, but the safest. Tell me something that only I will ever know, was perhaps what she wanted to ask him, or, What will you give me to remember you by?—or, even, Nothing of the least importance has ever belonged to me; can you help? Then she wondered if she had been foolish, or bold, amazed at her own thoughts, but he only stared down at the leaf he held in his hands and frowned a little, as one who devotes himself completely to an absorbing problem.

He is trying to phrase everything to make as good an impression as possible, she thought, and I will know how he holds me by what he answers; how is he anxious to appear to me? Does he think that I will be content with small mysticism, or will he exert himself to seem unique? Is he going to be gallant? That would be humiliating, because then he would show that he knows that gallantry enchants me; will he be mysterious? Mad? And how am I to receive this, which I perceive already will be a confidence, even if it is not true? Grant that Luke take me at my worth, she thought, or at least let me not see the difference. Let him be wise, or let me be blind; don't let me, she hoped concretely, don't let me know too surely what he thinks of me.

Then he looked at her briefly and smiled what she was

coming to know as his self-deprecatory smile; did Theodora, she wondered, and the thought was unwelcome, did Theodora know him as well as this?

"I never had a mother," he said, and the shock was enormous. Is *that* all he thinks of me, his estimate of what I want to hear of him; will I enlarge this into a confidence making me worthy of great confidences? Shall I sigh? Murmur? Walk away? "No one ever loved me because I belonged," he said. "I suppose you can understand that?"

No, she thought, you are not going to catch me so cheaply; I do not understand words and will not accept them in trade for my feelings; this man is a parrot. I will tell him that I can never understand such a thing, that maudlin self-pity does not move directly at my heart; I will not make a fool of myself by encouraging him to mock me. "I understand, yes," she said.

"I thought you might," he said, and she wanted, quite honestly, to slap his face. "I think you must be a very fine person, Nell," he said, and then spoiled it by adding, "warmhearted, and honest. Afterwards, when you go home . . ." His voice trailed off, and she thought, Either he is beginning to tell me something extremely important, or he is killing time until this conversation can gracefully be ended. He would not speak in this fashion without a reason; he does not willingly give himself away. Does he think that a human gesture of affection might seduce me into hurling myself madly at him? Is he afraid that I cannot behave like a lady? What does he know about me, about how I think and feel; does he feel sorry for me? "Journeys end in lovers meeting," she said.

"Yes," he said. "I never had a mother, as I told you. Now I find that everyone else has had something that I missed." He smiled at her. "I am entirely selfish," he said ruefully, "and always hoping that someone will tell me to behave, someone will make herself responsible for me and make me be grown-up."

He is altogether selfish, she thought in some surprise, the only man I have ever sat and talked to alone, and I am impatient; he is simply not very interesting. "Why don't you grow up by yourself?" she asked him, and wondered how many people—how many women—had already asked him that.

"You're clever." And how many times had he answered that way?

This conversation must be largely instinctive, she thought with amusement, and said gently, "You must be a very lonely person." All I want is to be cherished, she thought, and here I am talking gibberish with a selfish man. "You must be very lonely indeed."

He touched her hand, and smiled again. "You were so lucky," he told her. "You had a mother."

2

"I found it in the library," Luke said. "I swear I found it in the library."

"Incredible," the doctor said.

"Look," Luke said. He set the great book on the table and turned to the title page. "He made it himself—look, the title's been lettered in ink: MEMORIES, *for* SOPHIA ANNE LESTER CRAIN; *A Legacy for Her Education and Enlighten-*

ment During Her Lifetime From Her Affectionate and Devoted Father, HUGH DESMOND LESTER CRAIN; *Twenty-first June, 1881."*

They pressed around the table, Theodora and Eleanor and the doctor, while Luke lifted and turned the first great page of the book. "You see," Luke said, "his little girl is to learn humility. He has clearly cut up a number of fine old books to make this scrapbook, because I seem to recognize several of the pictures, and they are all glued in."

"The vanity of human accomplishment," the doctor said sadly. "Think of the books Hugh Crain hacked apart to make this. Now here is a Goya etching; a horrible thing for a little girl to meditate upon."

"Underneath he has written," Luke said, "under this ugly picture: 'Honor thy father and thy mother, Daughter, authors of thy being, upon whom a heavy charge has been laid, that they lead their child in innocence and righteousness along the fearful narrow path to everlasting bliss, and render her up at last to her God a pious and a virtuous soul; reflect, Daughter, upon the joy in Heaven as the souls of these tiny creatures wing upward, released before they have learned aught of sin or faithlessness, and make it thine unceasing duty to remain as pure as these.'"

"Poor baby," Eleanor said, and gasped as Luke turned the page; Hugh Crain's second moral lesson derived from a color plate of a snake pit, and vividly painted snakes writhed and twisted along the page, above the message, neatly printed, and touched with gold: "Eternal damnation is the lot of mankind; neither tears, nor reparation, can undo Man's heritage of sin. Daughter, hold apart from this world, that its lusts and ingratitudes corrupt thee not; Daughter, preserve thyself."

"Next comes hell," Luke said. "Don't look if you're squeamish."

"I think I will skip hell," Eleanor said, "but read it to me."

"Wise of you," the doctor said. "An illustration from Foxe; one of the less attractive deaths, I have always thought, although who can fathom the ways of martyrs?"

"See this, though," Luke said. "He's burnt away a corner of the page, and here is what he says: 'Daughter, could you but hear for a moment the agony, the screaming, the dreadful crying out and repentance, of those poor souls condemned to everlasting flame! Could thine eyes be seared, but for an instant, with the red glare of wasteland burning always! Alas, wretched beings, in undying pain! Daughter, your father has this minute touched the corner of his page to his candle, and seen the frail paper shrivel and curl in the flame; consider, Daughter, that the heat of this candle is to the everlasting fires of Hell as a grain of sand to the reaching desert, and, as this paper burns in its slight flame so shall your soul burn forever, in fire a thousandfold more keen.'"

"I'll bet he read it to her every night before she went to sleep," Theodora said.

"Wait," Luke said. "You haven't seen Heaven yet—even *you* can look at this one, Nell. It's Blake, and a bit stern, I think, but obviously better than Hell. Listen—'Holy, holy, holy! In the pure light of heaven the angels praise Him and one another unendingly. Daughter, it is Here that I will seek thee.'"

"What a labor of love it is," the doctor said. "Hours of time just planning it, and the lettering is so dainty, and the gilt—"

"Now the seven deadly sins," Luke said, "and I think the old boy drew them himself."

"He really put his heart into gluttony," Theodora said. "I'm not sure I'll ever be hungry again."

"Wait till lust," Luke told her. "The old fellow outdid himself."

"I don't really want to look at any more of it, I think," Theodora said. "I'll sit over here with Nell, and if you come across any particularly edifying moral precepts you think would do me good, read them aloud."

"*Here* is lust," Luke said. "Was ever woman in this humor wooed?"

"Good heavens," said the doctor. "Good heavens."

"He *must* have drawn it himself," Luke said.

"For a *child?*" The doctor was outraged.

"Her very own scrapbook. Note Pride, the very image of our Nell here."

"What?" said Eleanor, starting up.

"Teasing," the doctor said placatingly. "Don't come look, my dear; he's teasing you."

"Sloth, now," Luke said.

"Envy," said the doctor. "How the poor child dared transgress . . ."

"The last page is the very nicest, I think. This, ladies, is Hugh Crain's blood. Nell, do you want to see Hugh Crain's blood?"

"No, thank you."

"Theo? No? In any case, I insist, for the sake of your

two consciences, in reading what Hugh Crain has to say in closing his book: 'Daughter: sacred pacts are signed in blood, and I have here taken from my own wrist the vital fluid with which I bind you. Live virtuously, be meek, have faith in thy Redeemer, and in me, thy father, and I swear to thee that we will be joined together hereafter in unending bliss. Accept these precepts from thy devoted father, who in humbleness of spirit has made this book. May it serve its purpose well, my feeble effort, and preserve my Child from the pitfalls of this world and bring her safe to her father's arms in Heaven.' And signed: 'Thy everloving father, in this world and the next, author of thy being and guardian of thy virtue; in meekest love, Hugh Crain.' "

Theodora shuddered. "How he must have enjoyed it," she said, "signing his name in his own blood; I can see him laughing his head off."

"Not healthy, not at all a healthy work for a man," the doctor said.

"But she must have been very small when her father left the house," Eleanor said. "I wonder if he ever did read it to her."

"I'm sure he did, leaning over her cradle and spitting out the words so they would take root in her little mind. Hugh Crain," Theodora said, "you were a dirty old man, and you made a dirty old house and if you can still hear me from anywhere I would like to tell you to your face that I genuinely hope you will spend eternity in that foul horrible picture and never stop burning for a minute." She made a wild, derisive gesture around the room, and for a minute, still remembering, they were all silent, as though waiting for an answer, and then the coals in the fire fell

with a little crash, and the doctor looked at his watch and
Luke rose.

"The sun is over the yardarm," the doctor said happily.

3

Theodora curled by the fire, looking up wickedly at
Eleanor; at the other end of the room the chessmen moved
softly, jarring with little sounds against the table, and Theodora spoke gently, tormentingly. "Will you have him at
your little apartment, Nell, and offer him to drink from
your cup of stars?"

Eleanor looked into the fire, not answering. I have been
so silly, she thought, I have been a fool.

"Is there room enough for two? Would he come if you
asked him?"

Nothing could be worse than this, Eleanor thought; I
have been a fool.

"Perhaps he has been longing for a tiny home—something smaller, of course, than Hill House; perhaps he will
come home with you."

A fool, a ludicrous fool.

"Your white curtains—your tiny stone lions—"

Eleanor looked down at her, almost gently. "But I *had*
to come," she said, and stood up, turning blindly to get
away. Not hearing the startled voices behind her, not seeing where or how she went, she blundered somehow to the
great front door and out into the soft warm night. "I *had*
to come," she said to the world outside.

Fear and guilt are sisters; Theodora caught her on the
lawn. Silent, angry, hurt, they left Hill House side by side,
walking together, each sorry for the other. A person angry,

or laughing, or terrified, or jealous, will go stubbornly on into extremes of behavior impossible at another time; neither Eleanor nor Theodora reflected for a minute that it was imprudent for them to walk far from Hill House after dark. Each was so bent upon her own despair that escape into darkness was vital, and, containing themselves in that tight, vulnerable, impossible cloak which is fury, they stamped along together, each achingly aware of the other, each determined to be the last to speak.

Eleanor spoke first, finally; she had hurt her foot against a rock and tried to be too proud to notice it, but after a minute, her foot paining, she said, in a voice tight with the attempt to sound level, "I can't imagine why you think you have any right to interfere in my affairs," her language formal to prevent a flood of recrimination, or undeserved reproach (were they not strangers? cousins?). "I am sure that nothing I do is of any interest to you."

"That's right," Theodora said grimly. "Nothing that you do is of any interest to me."

We are walking on either side of a fence, Eleanor thought, but I have a right to live too, and I wasted an hour with Luke at the summerhouse trying to prove it. "I hurt my foot," she said.

"I'm sorry." Theodora sounded genuinely grieved. "You know what a beast he is." She hesitated. "A rake," she said finally, with a touch of amusement.

"I'm sure it's nothing to me *what* he is." And then, because they were women quarreling, "As if *you* cared, anyway."

"He shouldn't be allowed to get away with it," Theodora said.

"Get away with *what?*" Eleanor asked daintily.

"You're making a fool of yourself," Theodora said.

"Suppose I'm not, though? You'd mind terribly if you turned out to be wrong this time, wouldn't you?"

Theodora's voice was wearied, cynical. "If I'm wrong," she said, "I will bless you with all my heart. Fool that you are."

"You could hardly say anything else."

They were moving along the path toward the brook. In the darkness their feet felt that they were going downhill, and each privately and perversely accused the other of taking, deliberately, a path they had followed together once before in happiness.

"Anyway," Eleanor said, in a reasonable tone, "it doesn't mean anything to you, no matter what happens. Why should you care whether I make a fool of myself?"

Theodora was silent for a minute, walking in the darkness, and Eleanor was suddenly absurdly sure that Theodora had put out a hand to her, unseen. "Theo," Eleanor said awkwardly, "I'm no good at talking to people and saying things."

Theodora laughed. "What *are* you good at?" she demanded. "Running away?"

Nothing irrevocable had yet been spoken, but there was only the barest margin of safety left them; each of them moving delicately along the outskirts of an open question, and, once spoken, such a question—as "Do you love me?" —could never be answered or forgotten. They walked slowly, meditating, wondering, and the path sloped down from their feet and they followed, walking side by side in the most extreme intimacy of expectation; their feinting and hesitation done with, they could only await passively for resolution. Each knew, almost within a breath, what the other was thinking and wanting to say; each of them almost wept for the other. They perceived at the same moment the change in the path and each knew then the other's knowledge of it; Theodora took Eleanor's arm and, afraid to stop, they moved on slowly, close together, and ahead of them the path widened and blackened and curved.

Eleanor caught her breath, and Theodora's hand tightened, warning her to be quiet. On either side of them the trees, silent, relinquished the dark color they had held, paled, grew transparent and stood white and ghastly against the black sky. The grass was colorless, the path wide and black; there was nothing else. Eleanor's teeth were chattering, and the nausea of fear almost doubled her; her arm shivered under Theodora's holding hand, now almost a clutch, and she felt every slow step as a willed act, a precise mad insistence upon the putting of one foot down after the other as the only sane choice. Her eyes hurt with tears against the screaming blackness of the path and the shuddering whiteness of the trees, and she thought, with a clear intelligent picture of the words in her mind, burning, Now I am really afraid.

They moved on, the path unrolling ahead of them, the white trees unchanging on either side and, above all, the black sky lying thick overhead; their feet were shimmering white where they touched the path; Theodora's hand was pale and luminous. Ahead of them the path curved out of sight, and they walked slowly on, moving their feet precisely because it was the only physical act possible to them, the only thing left to keep them from sinking into the awful

blackness and whiteness and luminous evil glow. Now I
am really afraid, Eleanor thought in words of fire; remotely she could still feel Theodora's hand on her arm, but
Theodora was distant, locked away; it was bitterly cold,
with no human warmth near. Now I am really afraid, Eleanor thought, and put her feet forward one after another,
shivering as they touched the path, shivering with mindless cold.

The path unwound; perhaps it was taking them somewhere, willfully, since neither of them could step off it and
go knowingly into the annihilation of whiteness that was
the grass on either side. The path curved, black and shining, and they followed. Theodora's hand tightened, and
Eleanor caught her breath on a little sob—had something
moved, ahead, something whiter than the white trees, beckoning? Beckoning, fading into the trees, watching? Was
there movement beside them, imperceptible in the sound-
less night; did some footstep go invisibly along with them
in the white grass? Where were they?

The path led them to its destined end and died beneath
their feet. Eleanor and Theodora looked into a garden,
their eyes blinded with the light of sun and rich color; incredibly, there was a picnic party on the grass in the garden. They could hear the laughter of the children and the
affectionate, amused voices of the mother and father; the
grass was richly, thickly green, the flowers were colored
red and orange and yellow, the sky was blue and gold, and
one child wore a scarlet jumper and raised its voice again
in laughter, tumbling after a puppy over the grass. There
was a checked tablecloth spread out, and, smiling, the

mother leaned over to take up a plate of bright
Theodora screamed.

"Don't look back," she cried out in a voice
fear, "don't look back—don't look—run!"

Running, without knowing why she ran, Eleanor
thought that she would catch her foot in the checked tablecloth; she was afraid she might stumble over the puppy;
but as they ran across the garden there was nothing except
weeds growing blackly in the darkness, and Theodora,
screaming still, trampled over the bushes where there had
been flowers and stumbled, sobbing, over half-buried stones
and what might have been a broken cup. Then they were
beating and scratching wildly at the white stone wall where
vines grew blackly, screaming still and begging to be let
out, until a rusted iron gate gave way and they ran, crying
and gasping and somehow holding hands, across the
kitchen garden of Hill House, and crashed through a back
door into the kitchen to see Luke and the doctor hurrying
to them. "What happened?" Luke said, catching at Theodora. "Are you all right?"

"We've been nearly crazy," the doctor said, worn.
"We've been out looking for you for hours."

"It was a picnic," Eleanor said. She had fallen into a
kitchen chair and she looked down at her hands, scratched
and bleeding and shaking without her knowledge. "We
tried to get out," she told them, holding her hands out for
them to see. "It was a picnic. The children . . ."

Theodora laughed in a little continuing cry, laughing on
and on thinly, and said through her laughter, "I looked
back—I went and looked behind us . . ." and laughed on.

"The children . . . and a puppy . . ."

"Eleanor." Theodora turned wildly and put her head against Eleanor. "Eleanor," she said. "Eleanor."

And, holding Theodora, Eleanor looked up at Luke and the doctor, and felt the room rock madly, and time, as she had always known time, stop.

7

~~~~~~~~~~~~~~~~~~~~~~~~~~~~~~~~~~~

On THE afternoon of the day that Mrs. Montague
was expected, Eleanor went alone into the hills above Hill
House, not really intending to arrive at any place in particular, not even caring where or how she went, wanting
only to be secret and out from under the heavy dark wood
of the house. She found a small spot where the grass was
soft and dry and lay down, wondering how many years
it had been since she had lain on soft grass to be alone to
think. Around her the trees and wild flowers, with that
oddly courteous air of natural things suddenly interrupted

in their pressing occupations of growing and dying, turned toward her with attention, as though, dull and imperceptive as she was, it was still necessary for them to be gentle to a creation so unfortunate as not to be rooted in the ground, forced to go from one place to another, heart-breakingly mobile. Idly Eleanor picked a wild daisy, which died in her fingers, and, lying on the grass, looked up into its dead face. There was nothing in her mind beyond an overwhelming wild happiness. She pulled at the daisy, and wondered, smiling at herself, What am I going to do? What *am* I going to do?

2

"Put the bags down in the hall, Arthur," Mrs. Montague said. "Wouldn't you think there'd be someone here to help us with this door? They'll *have* to get someone to take the bags upstairs. John? John?"

"My dear, my dear." Dr. Montague hurried into the hallway, carrying his napkin, and kissed his wife obediently on the cheek she held out for him. "How nice that you got here; we'd given you up."

"I *said* I'd be here today, didn't I? Did you ever know me *not* to come when I said I would? I brought Arthur."

"Arthur," the doctor said without enthusiasm.

"Well, *some*body had to drive," Mrs. Montague said. "I imagine you expected that I would drive myself all the way out here? Because you know perfectly well that I get tired. How do you do."

The doctor turned, smiling on Eleanor and Theodora, with Luke behind them, clustered uncertainly in the doorway. "My dear," he said, "these are my friends who have been staying in Hill House with me these past few days. Theodora. Eleanor Vance. Luke Sanderson."

Theodora and Eleanor and Luke murmured civilly, and Mrs. Montague nodded and said, "I see you didn't bother to wait dinner for us."

"We'd given you up," the doctor said.

"I believe that I told you that I would be here today. Of course, it is *perfectly* possible that I am mistaken, but it is *my* recollection that I said I would be here today. I'm sure I will get to know all your names very soon. This gentleman is Arthur Parker; he drove me here because I dislike driving myself. Arthur, these are John's friends. Can anybody do something about our suitcases?"

The doctor and Luke approached, murmuring, and Mrs. Montague went on, "I am to be in your most haunted room, of course. Arthur can go anywhere. That blue suitcase is mine, young man, and the small attaché case; they will go in your most haunted room."

"The nursery, I think," Dr. Montague said when Luke looked at him inquiringly. "I believe the nursery is one source of disturbance," he told his wife, and she sighed irritably.

"It does seem to me that you could be more methodical," she said. "You've been here nearly a week and I suppose you've done *nothing* with planchette? Automatic writing? I don't imagine either of these young women has mediumistic gifts? Those are Arthur's bags right there. He brought his golf clubs, just in case."

"Just in case of what?" Theodora asked blankly, and Mrs. Montague turned to regard her coldly.

"Please don't let me interrupt your dinner," she said finally.

"There's a definite cold spot just outside the nursery door," the doctor told his wife hopefully.

"Yes, dear, very nice. Isn't that young man going to take Arthur's bags upstairs? You do seem to be in a good deal of confusion here, don't you? After nearly a week I certainly thought you'd have things in some kind of order. Any figures materialize?"

"There have been decided manifestations—"

"Well, I'm here now, and we'll get things going right. Where is Arthur to put the car?"

"There's an empty stable in back of the house where we have put our other cars. He can take it around in the morning."

"Nonsense. I do not believe in putting things off, John, as you know perfectly well. Arthur will have plenty to do in the morning without adding tonight's work. He must move the car at once."

"It's dark outside," the doctor said hesitantly.

"John, you astound me. Is it your belief that I do *not* know whether it is dark outside at night? The car has lights, John, and that young man can go with Arthur to show him the way."

"Thank you," said Luke grimly, "but we have a positive policy against going outside after dark. Arthur may, of course, if he cares to, but I will not."

"The young ladies," the doctor said, "had a shocking—"

"Young man's a coward," Arthur said. He had concluded his fetching of suitcases and golf bags and hampers from the car and now stood beside Mrs. Montague, looking down on Luke; Arthur's face was red and his hair was white, and now, scorning Luke, he bristled. "Ought to be ashamed of yourself, fellow, in front of the women."

"The women are just as much afraid as I am," Luke said primly.

"Indeed, indeed." Dr. Montague put his hand on Arthur's arm soothingly. "After you've been here for a while, Arthur, you'll understand that Luke's attitude is sensible, not cowardly. We make a point of staying together after dark."

"I must say, John, I never expected to find you all so *nervous*," Mrs. Montague said. "I deplore fear in these matters." She tapped her foot irritably. "You know perfectly well, John, that those who have passed beyond *expect* to see us happy and smiling; they *want* to know that we are thinking of them lovingly. The spirits dwelling in this house may be actually *suffering* because they are aware that you are afraid of them."

"We can talk about it later," the doctor said wearily. "Now, how about dinner?"

"Of course." Mrs. Montague glanced at Theodora and Eleanor. "What a pity that we had to interrupt you," she said.

"Have you had dinner?"

"Naturally we have not had dinner, John. I *said* we would be here for dinner, didn't I? Or am I mistaken again?"

"At any rate, I told Mrs. Dudley that you would be here," the doctor said, opening the door which led to the game room and on into the dining room. "She left us a splendid feast."

Poor Dr. Montague, Eleanor thought, standing aside to let the doctor take his wife into the dining room; he is so uncomfortable; I wonder how long she is going to stay.

"I wonder how long she is going to stay?" Theodora whispered in her ear.

"Maybe her suitcase is filled with ectoplasm," Eleanor said hopefully.

"And how long will you be able to stay?" Dr. Montague asked, sitting at the head of the dinner table with his wife cozily beside him.

"Well, dear," Mrs. Montague said, tasting daintily of Mrs. Dudley's caper sauce "—you have found a fair cook, have you not?—you *know* that Arthur has to get back to his school; Arthur is a headmaster," she explained down the table, "and he has generously canceled his appointments for Monday. So we had better leave Monday afternoon and then Arthur can be there for classes on Tuesday."

"A lot of happy schoolboys Arthur no doubt left behind," Luke said softly to Theodora, and Theodora said, "But today is only Saturday."

"I do not mind this cooking at all," Mrs. Montague said. "John, I will speak to your cook in the morning."

"Mrs. Dudley is an admirable woman," the doctor said carefully.

"Bit fancy for *my* taste," Arthur said. "I'm a meat-and-potatoes man, myself," he explained to Theodora. "Don't drink, don't smoke, don't read trash. Bad example for the fellows at the school. They look up to one a bit, you know."

"I'm sure they must all model themselves on you," Theodora said soberly.

"Get a bad hat now and then," Arthur said, shaking his head. "No taste for sports, you know. Moping in corners. Crybabies. Knock *that* out of them fast enough." He reached for the butter.

Mrs. Montague leaned forward to look down the table at Arthur. "Eat lightly, Arthur," she advised. "We have a busy night ahead of us."

"What on earth do you plan to do?" the doctor asked.

"I'm sure that *you* would never dream of going about these things with any system, but you will have to admit, John, that in this area I have simply more of an instinctive understanding; women do, you know, John, at least *some* women." She paused and regarded Eleanor and Theodora speculatively. "Neither of *them*, I daresay. Unless, of course, I am mistaken again? You are very fond of pointing out my errors, John."

"My dear—"

"I *cannot* abide a slipshod job in anything. Arthur will patrol, of course. I brought Arthur for that purpose. It is so rare," she explained to Luke, who sat on her other side, "to find persons in the educational field who are interested in the other world; you will find Arthur surprisingly well informed. I will recline in your haunted room with only a nightlight burning, and will endeavor to get in touch with the elements disturbing this house. I never sleep when there are troubled spirits about," she told Luke, who nodded, speechless.

"Little sound common sense," Arthur said. "Got to go about these things in the right way. Never pays to aim too low. Tell my fellows that."

"I think perhaps after dinner we will have a little session

with planchette," Mrs. Montague said. "Just Arthur and I, of course; the rest of you, I can see, are not ready yet; you would only drive away the spirits. We will need a quiet room—"

"The library," Luke suggested politely.

"The library? I think it might do; books are frequently very good carriers, you know. Materializations are often best produced in rooms where there are books. I cannot think of any time when materialization was in any way hampered by the presence of books. I suppose the library has been dusted? Arthur sometimes sneezes."

"Mrs. Dudley keeps the entire house in perfect order," the doctor said.

"I really will speak to Mrs. Dudley in the morning. You will show us the library, then, John, and that young man will bring down my case; not the large suitcase, mind, but the small attaché case. Bring it to me in the library. We will join you later; after a session with planchette I require a glass of milk and perhaps a small cake; crackers will do if they are not too heavily salted. A few minutes of quiet conversation with congenial people is also very helpful, particularly if I am to be receptive during the night; the mind is a precise instrument and cannot be tended too carefully. Arthur?" She bowed distantly to Eleanor and Theodora and went out, escorted by Arthur, Luke, and her husband.

After a minute Theodora said, "I think I am going to be simply crazy about Mrs. Montague."

"I don't know," Eleanor said. "Arthur is rather more to my taste. And Luke *is* a coward, I think."

"Poor Luke," Theodora said. "He never had a mother."

Looking up, Eleanor found that Theodora was regarding her with a curious smile, and she moved away from the table so quickly that a glass spilled.

"We shouldn't be alone," she said, oddly breathless. "We've got to find the others." She left the table and almost ran from the room, and Theodora ran after her, laughing, down the corridor and into the little parlor, where Luke and the doctor stood before the fire.

"Please, sir," Luke was saying meekly, "who is planchette?"

The doctor sighed irritably. "Imbeciles," he said, and then, "Sorry. The whole idea annoys me, but if *she* likes it . . ." He turned and poked the fire furiously. "Planchette," he went on after a moment, "is a device similar to the Ouija Board, or perhaps I might explain better by saying that it is a form of automatic writing; a method of communicating with—ah—intangible beings, although to *my* way of thinking the only intangible beings who ever get in touch through one of those things are the imaginations of the people running it. Yes. Well. Planchette is a little piece of light wood, usually heart-shaped or triangular. A pencil is set into the narrow end, and at the other end is a pair of wheels, or feet which will slip easily over paper. Two people place fingers on it, ask it questions, and the object moves, pushed by what force we will not here discuss, and writes answers. The Ouija Board, as I say, is very similar, except that the object moves on a board pointing to separate letters. An ordinary wineglass will do the same thing; I have seen it tried with a child's wheeled toy, although I will admit that it looked silly. Each person uses the tips of the fingers of one hand, keeping the other hand free to note down questions and answers. The answers are invariably, I believe, meaningless, although of course my wife will tell you different. Balderdash." And he went at the fire again. "Schoolgirls," he said. "Superstition."

3

"Planchette has been very kind tonight," Mrs. Montague said. "John, there are definitely foreign elements present in this house."

"Quite a splendid sitting, really," Arthur said. He waved a sheaf of paper triumphantly.

"We've gotten a good deal of information for you," Mrs. Montague said. "Now. Planchette was quite insistent about a nun. Have you learned anything about a nun, John?"

"In Hill House? Not likely."

"Planchette felt very strongly about a nun, John. Perhaps something of the sort—a dark, vague figure, even—has been seen in the neighborhood? Villagers terrified when staggering home late at night?"

"The figure of a nun is a fairly common—"

"John, if you please. I assume you are suggesting that I am mistaken. Or perhaps it is your intention to point out that *planchette* may be mistaken? I assure you—and you must believe planchette, even if *my* word is not good enough for you—that a nun was most specifically suggested."

"I am only trying to say, my dear, that the wraith of a nun is far and away the most common form of appearance. There has never been such a thing connected with Hill House, but in almost every—"

"John, *if* you *please*. I assume I may continue? Or is planchette to be dismissed without a hearing? Thank you." Mrs. Montague composed herself. "Now, then. There is also a name, spelled variously as Helen, or Helene, or Elena. Who might that be?"

"My dear, many people have lived—"

"Helen brought us a warning against a mysterious monk. Now when a monk and a nun *both* turn up in one house—"

"Expect the place was built on an older site," Arthur said. "Influences prevailing, you know. Older influences hanging around," he explained more fully.

"It sounds very much like broken vows, does it not? Very much."

"Had a lot of that back then, you know. Temptation, probably."

"I hardly think—" the doctor began.

"I daresay she was walled up alive," Mrs. Montague said. "The nun, I mean. They always did that, you know. You've no idea the messages I've gotten from nuns walled up alive."

"There is *no* case on record of *any* nun *ever* being—"

"John. May I point out to you once more that I *myself* have had messages from nuns walled up alive? Do you think I am telling you a fib, John? Or do you suppose that a nun would deliberately *pretend* to have been walled up alive when she was not? Is it possible that I am mistaken once more, John?"

"Certainly not, my dear." Dr. Montague sighed wearily.

"With one candle and a crust of bread," Arthur told Theodora. "Horrible thing to do, when you think about it."

"No nun was ever walled up alive," the doctor said sullenly. He raised his voice slightly. "It is a legend. A story. A libel circulated—"

"All right, John. We won't quarrel over it. You may believe whatever you choose. Just understand, however, that sometimes purely materialistic views must give way before *facts*. Now it is a proven fact that among the visitations troubling this house are a nun and a—"

"What else was there?" Luke asked hastily. "I am *so* interested in hearing what—ah—planchette had to say."

Mrs. Montague waggled a finger roguishly. "Nothing about *you*, young man. Although one of the ladies present may hear something of interest."

Impossible woman, Eleanor thought; impossible, vulgar, possessive woman. "Now, Helen," Mrs. Montague went on, "wants us to search the cellar for an old well."

"Don't tell me *Helen* was *buried* alive," the doctor said.

"I hardly think so, John. I am sure that she would have mentioned it. As a matter of fact, Helen was most unclear about just what we *were* to find in the well. I doubt, however, that it will be treasure. One so rarely meets with *real* treasure in a case of this kind. More likely evidence of the missing nun."

"More likely eighty years of rubbish."

"John, I can*not* understand this skepticism in you, of all people. After all, you did come to this house to collect evidence of supernatural activity, and now, when I bring you a full account of the *causes*, and an indication of where to start looking, you are positively scornful."

"We have no authority to dig up the cellar."

"Arthur could—" Mrs. Montague began hopefully, but the doctor said with firmness, "No. My lease of the house specifically forbids me to tamper with the house itself. There will be no digging of cellars, no tearing out of woodwork, no ripping up of floors. Hill House is still a valuable property, and we are students, not vandals."

"I should think you'd want to know the *truth*, John."

"There is nothing I should like to know more." Dr. Montague stamped across the room to the chessboard and took up a knight and regarded it furiously. He looked as though he were doggedly counting to a hundred.

"Dear me, how patient one must be sometimes." Mrs. Montague sighed. "But I do want to read you the little passage we received toward the end. Arthur, do you have it?"

Arthur shuffled through his sheaf of papers. "It was just after the message about the flowers you are to send to your aunt," Mrs. Montague said. "Planchette has a control named Merrigot," she explained, "and Merrigot takes a genuine personal interest in Arthur; brings him word from relatives, and so on."

"Not a fatal illness, you understand," Arthur said gravely. "Have to send flowers, of course, but Merrigot is most reassuring."

"Now." Mrs. Montague selected several pages, and turned them over quickly; they were covered with loose, sprawling penciled words, and Mrs. Montague frowned, running down the pages with her finger. "Here," she said. "Arthur, you read the questions and I'll read the answers; that way, it will sound more natural."

"Off we go," Arthur said brightly, and leaned over Mrs. Montague's shoulder. "Now—let me see—start right about here?"

"With 'Who are you?' "

"Righto. Who are you?"

"Nell," Mrs. Montague read in her sharp voice, and Eleanor and Theodora and Luke and the doctor turned, listening.

"Nell who?"

"Eleanor Nellie Nell Nell. They sometimes do that," Mrs. Montague broke off to explain. "They repeat a word over and over to make sure it comes across all right."

Arthur cleared his throat. "What do you want?" he read.

"Home."

"Do you want to go home?" And Theodora shrugged comically at Eleanor.

"Want to be home."

"What are you doing here?"

"Waiting."

"Waiting for what?"

"Home." Arthur stopped, and nodded profoundly. "There it is again," he said. "Like a word, and use it over and over, just for the sound of it."

"Ordinarily we never ask *why*," Mrs. Montague said, "because it tends to confuse planchette. However, this time we were bold, and came right out and asked. Arthur?"

"Why?" Arthur read.

"Mother," Mrs. Montague read. "So you see, this time we were right to ask, because planchette was perfectly free with the answer."

"Is Hill House your home?" Arthur read levelly.

"Home," Mrs. Montague responded, and the doctor sighed.

"Are you suffering?" Arthur read.

"No answer here." Mrs. Montague nodded reassuringly. "Sometimes they dislike admitting to pain; it tends to discourage those of us left behind, you know. Just like Arthur's aunt, for instance, will *never* let on that she is sick, but Merrigot always lets us know, and it's even worse when they've passed over."

"Stoical," Arthur confirmed, and read, "Can we help you?"

"No," Mrs. Montague read.

"Can we do anything at all for you?"

"No. Lost. Lost. Lost." Mrs. Montague looked up. "You see?" she asked. "One word, over and over again. They *love* to repeat themselves. I've had one word go on to cover a whole page sometimes."

"What do you want?" Arthur read.

"Mother," Mrs. Montague read back.

"Why?"

"Child."

"Where is your mother?"

"Home."

"Where is your home?"

"Lost. Lost. Lost. And after that," Mrs. Montague said, folding the paper briskly, "there was nothing but gibberish."

"*Never* known planchette so cooperative," Arthur said confidingly to Theodora. "Quite an experience, really."

"But why pick on Nell?" Theodora asked with annoyance. "Your fool planchette has no right to send messages to people without permission or—"

"You'll never get results by abusing planchette," Arthur

began, but Mrs. Montague interrupted him, swinging to stare at Eleanor. "*You*'re Nell?" she demanded, and turned on Theodora. "We thought *you* were Nell," she said.

"So?" said Theodora impudently.

"It doesn't affect the messages, of course," Mrs. Montague said, tapping her paper irritably, "although I *do* think we might have been correctly introduced. I am sure that *planchette* knew the difference between you, but I certainly do not care to be misled."

"Don't feel neglected," Luke said to Theodora. "We will bury you alive."

"When I get a message from that thing," Theodora said, "I expect it to be about hidden treasure. None of this nonsense about sending flowers to my aunt."

They are all carefully avoiding looking at me, Eleanor thought; I have been singled out again, and they are kind enough to pretend it is nothing; "Why do you think all that was sent to me?" she asked, helpless.

"Really, child," Mrs. Montague said, dropping the papers on the low table, "I couldn't *begin* to say. Although you *are* rather more than a child, aren't you? Perhaps you are more receptive psychically than you realize, although"—and she turned away indifferently—"how you *could* be, a week in this house and not picking up the simplest message from beyond . . . That fire wants stirring."

"Nell doesn't want messages from beyond," Theodora said comfortingly, moving to take Eleanor's cold hand in hers. "Nell wants her warm bed and a little sleep."

Peace, Eleanor thought concretely; what I want in all

this world is peace, a quiet spot to lie and think, a quiet spot up among the flowers where I can dream and tell myself sweet stories.

4

"I," Arthur said richly, "shall make my headquarters in the small room just this side of the nursery, well within shouting distance. I shall have with me a drawn revolver—do not take alarm, ladies; I am an excellent shot—and a flashlight, in addition to a most piercing whistle. I shall have no difficulty summoning the rest of you in case I observe anything worth your notice, or I require—ah—company. You may all sleep quietly, I assure you."

"Arthur," Mrs. Montague explained, "will patrol the house. Every hour, regularly, he will make a round of the upstairs rooms; I think he need hardly bother with the downstairs rooms tonight, since *I* shall be up here. We have done this before, many times. Come along, everyone." Silently they followed her up the staircase, watching her little affectionate dabs at the stair rail and the carvings on the walls. "It is such a blessing," she said once, "to know that the beings in this house are only waiting for an opportunity to tell their stories and free themselves from the burden of their sorrow. Now. Arthur will first of all inspect the bedrooms. Arthur?"

"With apologies, ladies, with apologies," Arthur said, opening the door of the blue room, which Eleanor and Theodora shared. "A dainty spot," he said plummily, "fit for two such charming ladies; I shall, if you like, save you the trouble of glancing into the closet and under the bed."

Solemnly they watched Arthur go down onto his hands and knees and look under the beds and then rise, dusting his hands. "Perfectly safe," he said.

"Now, where am I to be?" Mrs. Montague asked. "Where did that young man put my bags?"

"Directly at the end of the hall," the doctor said. "We call it the nursery."

Mrs. Montague, followed by Arthur, moved purposefully down the hall, passed the cold spot in the hall, and shivered. "I will certainly need extra blankets," she said. "Have that young man bring extra blankets from one of the other rooms." Opening the nursery door, she nodded and said, "The bed looks quite fresh, I must admit, but has the room been aired?"

"I told Mrs. Dudley," the doctor said.

"It smells musty. Arthur, you will have to open that window, in spite of the cold."

Drearily the animals on the nursery wall looked down on Mrs. Montague. "Are you sure . . ." The doctor hesitated, and glanced up apprehensively at the grinning faces over the nursery door. "I wonder if you ought to have someone in here with you," he said.

"My dear." Mrs. Montague, good-humored now in the presence of those who had passed beyond, was amused. "How many hours—how many, *many* hours—have I sat in purest love and understanding, alone in a room and yet never alone? My dear, how can I make you perceive that there is no danger where there is nothing but love and sympathetic understanding? I am here to *help* these unfortunate beings—I am here to extend the hand of heartfelt fondness, and let them know that there are still *some* who remember, who will listen and weep for them; their loneliness is over, and I—"

"Yes," the doctor said, "but leave the door open."

"Unlocked, if you insist." Mrs. Montague was positively magnanimous.

"I shall be only down the hall," the doctor said. "I can hardly offer to patrol, since that will be Arthur's occupation, but if you need anything I can hear you."

Mrs. Montague laughed and waved her hand at him. "These others need your protection so much more than I," she said. "I will do what I can, of course. But they are so very, *very* vulnerable, with their hard hearts and their unseeing eyes."

Arthur, followed by a Luke looking very much amused, returned from checking the other bedrooms on the floor and nodded briskly at the doctor. "All clear," he said. "Perfectly safe for you to go to bed now."

"Thank you," the doctor told him soberly and then said to his wife, "Good night. Be careful."

"Good night," Mrs. Montague said, and smiled around at all of them. "Please don't be afraid," she said. "No matter what happens, remember that I am here."

"Good night," Theodora said, and "Good night," said Luke, and with Arthur behind them assuring them that they might rest quietly, and not to worry if they heard shots, and he would start his first patrol at midnight, Eleanor and Theodora went into their own room, and Luke on down the hall to his. After a moment the doctor, turning reluctantly away from his wife's closed door, followed.

"Wait," Theodora said to Eleanor, once in their room. "Luke said they want us down the hall; don't get undressed and be quiet." She opened the door a crack and whispered over her shoulder, "I swear that old biddy's going to blow this house wide open with that perfect love business; if I ever saw a place that had no use for perfect love, it's Hill House. Now. Arthur's closed his door. Quick. Be quiet."

Silently, making no sound on the hall carpeting, they hurried in their stocking feet down the hall to the doctor's room. "Hurry," the doctor said, opening the door just wide enough for them to come in, "be quiet."

"It's not safe," Luke said, closing the door to a crack and coming back to sit on the floor, "that man's going to shoot somebody."

"I don't like it," the doctor said, worried. "Luke and I will stay up and watch, and I want you two ladies in here where we can keep an eye on you. Something's going to happen," he said. "I don't like it."

"I just hope she didn't go and make anything mad, with her planchette," Theodora said. "Sorry, Doctor Montague. I don't intend to speak rudely of your wife."

The doctor laughed, but stayed with his eye to the door. "She originally planned to come for our entire stay," he said, "but she had enrolled in a course in yoga and could not miss her meetings. She is an excellent woman in most respects," he added, looking earnestly around at them. "She is a good wife, and takes very good care of me. She does things splendidly, really. Buttons on my shirts." He smiled hopefully. "This"—and he gestured in the direction of the hall—"*this* is practically her only vice."

"Perhaps she feels she is helping you with your work," Eleanor said.

The doctor grimaced, and shivered; at that moment the

door swung wide and then crashed shut, and in the silence outside they could hear slow rushing movements as though a very steady, very strong wind were blowing the length of the hall. Glancing at one another, they tried to smile, tried to look courageous under the slow coming of the unreal cold and then, through the noise of wind, the knocking on the doors downstairs. Without a word Theodora took up the quilt from the foot of the doctor's bed and folded it around Eleanor and herself, and they moved close together, slowly in order not to make a sound. Eleanor, clinging to Theodora, deadly cold in spite of Theodora's arms around her, thought, It knows my name, it knows my name this time. The pounding came up the stairs, crashing on each step. The doctor was tense, standing by the door, and Luke moved over to stand beside him. "It's nowhere near the nursery," he said to the doctor, and put his hand out to stop the doctor from opening the door.

"How weary one gets of this constant pounding," Theodora said ridiculously. "Next summer, I must really go somewhere else."

"There are disadvantages everywhere," Luke told her. "In the lake regions you get mosquitoes."

"Could we have exhausted the repertoire of Hill House?" Theodora asked, her voice shaking in spite of her light tone. "Seems like we've had this pounding act before; is it going to start everything all over again?" The crashing echoed along the hall, seeming to come from the far end, the farthest from the nursery, and the doctor, tense against the door, shook his head anxiously. "I'm going to have to go out there," he said. "She might be frightened," he told them.

Eleanor, rocking to the pounding, which seemed inside her head as much as in the hall, holding tight to Theodora, said, "They know where we are," and the others, assuming that she meant Arthur and Mrs. Montague, nodded and listened. The knocking, Eleanor told herself, pressing her hands to her eyes and swaying with the noise, will go on down the hall, it will go on and on to the end of the hall and turn and come back again, it will just go on and on the way it did before and then it will stop and we will look at each other and laugh and try to remember how cold we were, and the little swimming curls of fear on our backs; after a while it will stop.

"It never hurt *us*," Theodora was telling the doctor, across the noise of the pounding. "It won't hurt *them*."

"I only hope she doesn't try to *do* anything about it," the doctor said grimly; he was still at the door, but seemingly unable to open it against the volume of noise outside.

"I feel positively like an old hand at this," Theodora said to Eleanor. "Come closer, Nell; keep warm," and she pulled Eleanor even nearer to her under the blanket, and the sickening, still cold surrounded them.

Then there came, suddenly, quiet, and the secret creeping silence they all remembered; holding their breaths, they looked at one another. The doctor held the doorknob with both hands, and Luke, although his face was white and his voice trembled, said lightly, "Brandy, anyone? My passion for spirits—"

"No." Theodora giggled wildly. "Not that pun," she said.

"Sorry. You won't believe me," Luke said, the brandy decanter rattling against the glass as he tried to pour, "but

I no longer think of it as a pun. That is what living in a haunted house does for a sense of humor." Using both hands to carry the glass, he came to the bed where Theodora and Eleanor huddled under the blanket, and Theodora brought out one hand and took the glass. "Here," she said, holding it to Eleanor's mouth. "Drink."

Sipping, not warmed, Eleanor thought, We are in the eye of the storm; there is not much more time. She watched Luke carefully carry a glass of brandy over to the doctor and hold it out, and then, without comprehending, watched the glass slip through Luke's fingers to the floor as the door was shaken, violently and silently. Luke pulled the doctor back, and the door was attacked without sound, seeming almost to be pulling away from its hinges, almost ready to buckle and go down, leaving them exposed. Backing away, Luke and the doctor waited, tense and helpless.

"It can't get in," Theodora was whispering over and over, her eyes on the door, "it can't get in, don't let it get in, it can't get in—" The shaking stopped, the door was quiet, and a little caressing touch began on the doorknob, feeling intimately and softly and then, because the door was locked, patting and fondling the doorframe, as though wheedling to be let in.

"It knows we're here," Eleanor whispered, and Luke, looking back at her over his shoulder, gestured furiously for her to be quiet.

It is so cold, Eleanor thought childishly; I will never be able to sleep again with all this noise coming from inside my head; how can these others hear the noise when it is coming from inside my head? I am disappearing inch by inch into this house, I am going apart a little bit at a time because all this noise is breaking me; why are the *others* frightened?

She was aware, dully, that the pounding had begun again, the metallic overwhelming sound of it washed over her like waves; she put her cold hands to her mouth to feel if her face was still there; I have had enough, she thought, I am too cold.

"At the nursery door," Luke said tensely, speaking clearly through the noise. "At the nursery door; don't." And he put out a hand to stop the doctor.

"Purest love," Theodora said madly, "purest love." And she began to giggle again.

"If they don't open the doors—" Luke said to the doctor. The doctor stood now with his head against the door, listening, with Luke holding his arm to keep him from moving.

Now we are going to have a new noise, Eleanor thought, listening to the inside of her head; it is changing. The pounding had stopped, as though it had proved ineffectual, and there was now a swift movement up and down the hall, as of an animal pacing back and forth with unbelievable impatience, watching first one door and then another, alert for a movement inside, and there was again the little babbling murmur which Eleanor remembered; Am I doing it? she wondered quickly, is that me? And heard the tiny laughter beyond the door, mocking her.

"Fe-fi-fo-fum," Theodora said under her breath, and the laughter swelled and became a shouting; it's inside my head, Eleanor thought, putting her hands over her face, it's inside my head and it's getting out, getting out, getting out—

Now the house shivered and shook, the curtains dashing

against the windows, the furniture swaying, and the noise in the hall became so great that it pushed against the walls; they could hear breaking glass as the pictures in the hall came down, and perhaps the smashing of windows. Luke and the doctor strained against the door, as though desperately holding it shut, and the floor moved under their feet. We're going, we're going, Eleanor thought, and heard Theodora say, far away, "The house is coming down." She sounded calm, and beyond fear. Holding to the bed, buffeted and shaken, Eleanor put her head down and closed her eyes and bit her lips against the cold and felt the sickening drop as the room fell away beneath her and then right itself and then turned, slowly, swinging. "God almighty," Theodora said, and a mile away at the door Luke caught the doctor and held him upright.

"Are you all right?" Luke called, back braced against the door, holding the doctor by the shoulders. "Theo, are you all right?"

"Hanging on," Theodora said. "I don't know about Nell."

"Keep her warm," Luke said, far away. "We haven't seen it all yet." His voice trailed away; Eleanor could hear and see him far away in the distant room where he and Theodora and the doctor still waited; in the churning darkness where she fell endlessly nothing was real except her own hands white around the bedpost. She could see them, very small, and see them tighten when the bed rocked and the wall leaned forward and the door turned sideways far away. Somewhere there was a great, shaking crash as some huge thing came headlong; it must be the tower, Eleanor thought, and I supposed it would stand for years; we are lost, lost; the house is destroying itself. She heard the laughter over all, coming thin and lunatic, rising in its little crazy tune, and thought, No; it is over for me. It is too much, she thought, I will relinquish my possession of this self of mine, abdicate, give over willingly what I never wanted at all; whatever it wants of me it can have.

"I'll come," she said aloud, and was speaking up to Theodora, who leaned over her. The room was perfectly quiet, and between the still curtains at the window she could see the sunlight. Luke sat in a chair by the window; his face was bruised and his shirt was torn, and he was still drinking brandy. The doctor sat back in another chair; his hair freshly combed, looking neat and dapper and self-possessed. Theodora, leaning over Eleanor, said, "She's all right, I think," and Eleanor sat up and shook her head, staring. Composed and quiet, the house lifted itself primly around her, and nothing had been moved.

"How . . ." Eleanor said, and all three of them laughed.

"Another day," the doctor said, and in spite of his appearance his voice was wan. "Another night," he said.

"As I tried to say earlier," Luke remarked, "living in a haunted house plays hell with a sense of humor; I really did not intend to make a forbidden pun," he told Theodora.

"How—are they?" Eleanor asked, the words sounding unfamiliar and her mouth stiff.

"Both sleeping like babies," the doctor said. "Actually," he said, as though continuing a conversation begun while Eleanor slept, "I cannot believe that my wife stirred up that storm, but I do admit that one more word about pure love . . ."

"What happened?" Eleanor asked; I must have been gritting my teeth all night, she thought, the way my mouth feels.

"Hill House went dancing," Theodora said, "taking us along on a mad midnight fling. At least, I *think* it was dancing; it might have been turning somersaults."

"It's almost nine," the doctor said. "When Eleanor is ready . . ."

"Come along, baby," Theodora said. "Theo will wash your face for you and make you all neat for breakfast."

8

~~~~~~

DID anyone tell them that Mrs. Dudley clears at ten?"
Theodora looked into the coffee pot speculatively.

The doctor hesitated. "I hate to wake them after such a
night."

"But Mrs. Dudley clears at ten."

"They're coming," Eleanor said. "I can hear them on the
stairs." I can hear everything, all over the house, she wanted
to tell them.

Then, distantly, they could all hear Mrs. Montague's
voice, raised in irritation and Luke, realizing, said, "Oh,

Lord—they can't find the dining room," and hurried out to open doors.

"—properly aired." Mrs. Montague's voice preceded her, and she swept into the dining room, tapped the doctor curtly on the shoulder by way of greeting and seated herself with a general nod to the others. "I must say," she began at once, "that I think you might have called us for breakfast. I suppose everything is cold? Is the coffee bearable?"

"Good morning," Arthur said sulkily, and sat down himself with an air of sullen ill temper. Theodora almost upset the coffee pot in her haste to set a cup of coffee before Mrs. Montague.

"It *seems* hot enough," Mrs. Montague said. "I shall speak to your Mrs. Dudley this morning in any case. That room must be aired."

"And your night?" the doctor asked timidly. "Did you spend a—ah—profitable night?"

"If by profitable you meant comfortable, John, I wish you would say so. No, in answer to your most civil inquiry, I did *not* spend a comfortable night. I did not sleep a wink. That room is unendurable."

"Noisy old house, isn't it?" Arthur said. "Branch kept tapping against my window all night; nearly drove me crazy, tapping and tapping."

"Even with the windows open that room is stuffy. Mrs. Dudley's coffee is not as poor as her housekeeping. Another cup, if you please. I am astonished, John, that you put me in a room not properly aired; if there is to be any communication with those beyond, the air circulation, at least, ought to be adequate. I smelled dust all night."

"Can't understand *you*," Arthur said to the doctor, "letting yourself get all nervy about this place. Sat there all night long with my revolver and not a mouse stirred. Except for that infernal branch tapping on the window. Nearly drove me crazy," he confided to Theodora.

"We will not give up hope, of course." Mrs. Montague scowled at her husband. "Perhaps tonight there may be some manifestations."

2

"Theo?" Eleanor put down her notepad, and Theodora, scribbling busily, looked up with a frown. "I've been thinking about something."

"I *hate* writing these notes; I feel like a damn fool trying to write this crazy stuff."

"I've been wondering."

"Well?" Theodora smiled a little. "You look so serious," she said. "Are you coming to some great decision?"

"Yes," Eleanor said, deciding. "About what I'm going to do afterwards. After we all leave Hill House."

"Well?"

"I'm coming with you," Eleanor said.

"Coming where with me?"

"Back with you, back home. I"—and Eleanor smiled wryly—"am going to follow you home."

Theodora stared. "Why?" she asked blankly.

"I never had anyone to care about," Eleanor said, wondering where she had heard someone say something like this before. "I want to be someplace where I belong."

"I am not in the habit of taking home stray cats," Theodora said lightly.

Eleanor laughed too. "I *am* a kind of stray cat, aren't I?"

"Well." Theodora took up her pencil again. "You have your own home," she said. "You'll be glad enough to get back to it when the time comes, Nell my Nellie. I suppose we'll all be glad to get back home. What are you saying about those noises last night? *I* can't describe them."

"I'll come, you know," Eleanor said. "I'll just come."

"Nellie, Nellie." Theodora laughed again. "Look," she said. "This is just a summer, just a few weeks' visit to a lovely old summer resort in the country. You have your life back home, I have *my* life. When the summer is over, we go back. We'll write each other, of course, and maybe visit, but Hill House is not forever, you know."

"I can get a job; I won't be in your way."

"I don't understand." Theodora threw down her pencil in exasperation. "Do you *always* go where you're not wanted?"

Eleanor smiled placidly. "I've never been wanted *anywhere*," she said.

3

"It's all so motherly," Luke said. "Everything so soft. Everything so padded. Great embracing chairs and sofas which turn out to be hard and unwelcome when you sit down, and reject you at once—"

"Theo?" Eleanor said softly, and Theodora looked at her and shook her head in bewilderment.

"—and hands everywhere. Little soft glass hands, curving out to you, beckoning—"

"Theo?" Eleanor said.

"No," Theodora said. "I won't have you. And I don't want to talk about it any more."

"Perhaps," Luke said, watching them, "the single most repulsive aspect is the emphasis upon the globe. I ask you to regard impartially the lampshade made of tiny pieces of broken glass glued together, or the great round balls of the lights upon the stairs or the fluted iridescent candy jar at Theo's elbow. In the dining room there is a bowl of particularly filthy yellow glass resting upon the cupped hands of a child, and an Easter egg of sugar with a vision of shepherds dancing inside. A bosomy lady supports the stair-rail on her head, and under glass in the drawing room—"

"Nellie, leave me alone. Let's walk down to the brook or something."

"—a child's face, done in cross-stitch. Nell, don't look so apprehensive; Theo has only suggested that you walk down to the brook. If you like, I will go along."

"Anything," Theodora said.

"To frighten away rabbits. If you like, I will carry a stick. If you like, I will not come at all. Theo has only to say the word."

Theodora laughed. "Perhaps Nell would rather stay here and write on walls."

"So unkind," Luke said. "Callous of you, Theo."

"I want to hear more about the shepherds dancing in the Easter egg," Theodora said.

"A world contained in sugar. Six very tiny shepherds dancing, and a shepherdess in pink and blue reclining upon a mossy bank enjoying them; there are flowers and trees and sheep, and an old goatherd playing pipes. I would like to have been a goatherd, I think."

"If you were not a bullfighter," Theodora said.

"If I were not a bullfighter. Nell's affairs are the talk of the cafés, you will recall."

"Pan," Theodora said. "You should live in a hollow tree, Luke."

"Nell," Luke said, "you are not listening."

"I think you frighten her, Luke."

"Because Hill House will be mine someday, with its untold treasures and its cushions? I am not gentle with a house, Nell; I might take a fit of restlessness and smash the sugar Easter egg, or shatter the little child hands or go stomping and shouting up and down the stairs striking at glued-glass lamps with a cane and slashing at the bosomy lady with the staircase on her head; I might—"

"You see? You do frighten her."

"I believe I do," Luke said. "Nell, I am only talking nonsense."

"I don't think he even owns a cane," Theodora said.

"As a matter of fact, I do. Nell, I am *only* talking nonsense. What is she thinking about, Theo?"

Theodora said carefully, "She wants me to take her home with me after we leave Hill House, and I won't do it."

Luke laughed. "Poor silly Nell," he said. "Journeys end in lovers meeting. Let's go down to the brook."

"A mother house," Luke said, as they came down the steps from the veranda to the lawn, "a housemother, a headmistress, a housemistress. I am sure I will be a very poor housemaster, like our Arthur, when Hill House belongs to me."

"I can't understand anyone wanting to own Hill House," Theodora said, and Luke turned and looked back with amusement at the house.

"You never know what you are going to want until you see it clearly," he said. "If I never had a chance of owning it I might feel very differently. What do people really want with each other, as Nell asked me once; what use are other people?"

"It was my fault my mother died," Eleanor said. "She knocked on the wall and called me and called me and I never woke up. I ought to have brought her the medicine; I always did before. But this time she called me and I never woke up."

"You should have forgotten all that by now," Theodora said.

"I've wondered ever since if I did wake up. If I did wake up and hear her, and if I just went back to sleep. It would have been easy, and I've wondered about it."

"Turn here," Luke said. "If we're going to the brook."

"You worry too much, Nell. You probably just *like* thinking it was your fault."

"It was going to happen sooner or later, in any case," Eleanor said. "But of course no matter when it happened, it was going to be my fault."

"If it hadn't happened you would never have come to Hill House."

"We go single file along here," Luke said. "Nell, go first."

Smiling, Eleanor went on ahead, kicking her feet comfortably along the path. Now I know where I am going, she thought; I told her about my mother so *that's* all right; I will find a little house, or maybe an apartment like hers. I will see her every day, and we will go searching together for lovely things—gold-trimmed dishes, and a white cat, and a sugar Easter egg, and a cup of stars. I will not be frightened or alone any more; I will call myself just *Eleanor.* "Are you two talking about me?" she asked over her shoulder.

After a minute Luke answered politely, "A struggle between good and evil for the soul of Nell. I suppose I will have to be God, however."

"But of course she can*not* trust either of us," Theodora said, amused.

"Not me, certainly," Luke said.

"Besides, Nell," Theodora said, "we were not talking about you at all. As though I were the games mistress," she said, half angry, to Luke.

I have waited such a long time, Eleanor was thinking; I have finally earned my happiness. She came, leading them, to the top of the hill and looked down to the slim line of trees they must pass through to get to the brook. They are lovely against the sky, she thought, so straight and free; Luke was wrong about the softness everywhere, because the trees are hard like wooden trees. They are still talking about me, talking about how I came to Hill House and found Theodora and now I will not let her go. Behind her she could hear the murmur of their voices, edged sometimes with malice, sometimes rising in mockery, sometimes touched with a laughter almost of kinship, and she walked on dreamily, hearing them come behind. She could tell when they entered the tall grass a minute after she did, because the grass moved hissingly beneath their feet and a startled grasshopper leaped wildly away.

I could help her in her shop, Eleanor thought; she loves beautiful things and I would go with her to find them. We could go anywhere we pleased, to the edge of the world if we liked, and come back when we wanted to. He is telling her now what he knows about me: that I am not easily taken in, that I had an oleander wall around me, and she is laughing because I am not going to be lonely any more. They are very much alike and they are very kind; I would not really have expected as much from them as they are giving me; I was very right to come because journeys end in lovers meeting.

She came under the hard branches of the trees and the shadows were pleasantly cool after the hot sun on the path; now she had to walk more carefully because the path led downhill and there were sometimes rocks and roots across her way. Behind her their voices went on, quick and sharp, and then more slowly and laughing; I will not look back, she thought happily, because then they would know what I am thinking; we will talk about it together someday, Theo and I, when we have plenty of time. How strange I feel, she thought, coming out of the trees onto the last steep part of the path going down to the brook; I am caught in a kind of wonder, I am still with joy. I will not look around until I am next to the brook, where she almost fell the day we came; I will remind her about the golden fish in the brook and about our picnic.

She sat down on the narrow green bank and put her chin on her knees; I will not forget this one moment in my life, she promised herself, listening to their voices and their footsteps coming slowly down the hill. "Hurry up," she said, turning her head to look for Theodora. "I—" and was silent. There was no one on the hill, nothing but the footsteps coming clearly along the path and the faint mocking laughter.

"Who—?" she whispered. "Who?"

She could see the grass go down under the weight of the footsteps. She saw another grasshopper leap wildly away, and a pebble jar and roll. She heard clearly the brush of footsteps on the path and then, standing back hard against the bank, heard the laughter very close; "Eleanor, Eleanor," and she heard it inside and outside her head; this was a call she had been listening for all her life. The footsteps stopped and she was caught in a movement of air so solid that she staggered and was held. "Eleanor, Eleanor," she heard through the rushing of air past her ears, "Eleanor, Eleanor," and she was held tight and safe. It is not cold at all, she thought, it is not cold at all. She closed her eyes and leaned back against the bank and thought, Don't let me go, and then, Stay, stay, as the firmness which held her slipped away, leaving her and fading; "Eleanor, Eleanor," she heard once more and then she stood beside the brook, shivering as though the sun had gone, watching without surprise the vacant footsteps move across the water of the brook, sending small ripples going, and then over onto the grass on the other side, moving slowly and caressingly up and over the hill.

Come back, she almost said, standing shaking by the brook, and then she turned and ran madly up the hill, crying as she ran and calling, "Theo? Luke?"

She found them in the little group of trees, leaning against a tree trunk and talking softly and laughing; when she ran to them they turned, startled, and Theodora was almost angry. "What on earth do you want this time?" she said.

"I waited for you by the brook—"

"We decided to stay here where it was cool," Theodora said. "We thought you heard us calling you. Didn't we, Luke?"

"Oh, yes," said Luke, embarrassed. "We were sure you heard us calling."

"Anyway," Theodora said, "we were going to come along in a minute. Weren't we, Luke?"

"Yes," said Luke, grinning. "Oh, yes."

4

"Subterranean waters," the doctor said, waving his fork.

"Nonsense. Does Mrs. Dudley do all your cooking? The asparagus is more than passable. Arthur, let that young man help you to asparagus."

"My dear." The doctor looked fondly upon his wife. "It has become our custom to rest for an hour or so after lunch; if you—"

"Certainly not. I have far too much to do while I am here. I must speak to your cook, I must see that my room is aired, I must ready planchette for another session this evening; Arthur must clean his revolver."

"Mark of a fighting man," Arthur conceded. "Firearms always in good order."

"*You* and *these* young people may rest, of course. Perhaps you do not feel the urgency which I do, the terrible compulsion to aid whatever poor souls wander restlessly here; perhaps you find me foolish in my sympathy for them, perhaps I am even ludicrous in your eyes because I can spare a tear for a lost abandoned soul, left without any helping hand; pure love—"

"Croquet?" Luke said hastily. "Croquet, perhaps?" He looked eagerly from one to another. "Badminton?" he suggested. "Croquet?"

"Subterranean waters?" Theodora added helpfully.

"No fancy sauces for *me*," Arthur said firmly. "Tell my fellows it's the mark of a cad." He looked thoughtfully at Luke. "Mark of a cad. Fancy sauces, women waiting on you. *My* fellows wait on themselves. Mark of a man," he said to Theodora.

"And what else do you teach them?" Theodora asked politely.

"Teach? You mean—do they learn anything, my fellows? You mean—algebra, like? Latin? Certainly." Arthur sat back, pleased. "Leave all that kind of thing to the teachers," he explained.

"And how many fellows are there in your school?" Theodora leaned forward, courteous, interested, making conversation with a guest, and Arthur basked; at the head of the table Mrs. Montague frowned and tapped her fingers impatiently.

"How many? How many. Got a crack tennis team, you know." He beamed on Theodora. "Crack. Absolutely tophole. Not counting milksops?"

"Not counting," said Theodora, "milksops."

"Oh. Tennis. Golf. Baseball. Track. Cricket." He smiled

slyly. "Didn't guess we played cricket, did you? Then there's swimming, and volleyball. Some fellows go out for everything, though," he told her anxiously. "All-around types. Maybe seventy, altogether."

"Arthur?" Mrs. Montague could contain herself no longer. "No shop talk, now. You're on vacation, remember."

"Yes, silly of me." Arthur smiled fondly. "Got to check the weapons," he explained.

"It's two o'clock," Mrs. Dudley said in the doorway. "I clear off at two."

5

Theodora laughed, and Eleanor, hidden deep in the shadows behind the summerhouse, put her hands over her mouth to keep from speaking to let them know she was there; I've got to find out, she was thinking, I've got to find out.

"It's called 'The Grattan Murders,'" Luke was saying. "Lovely thing. I can even sing it if you prefer."

"Mark of a cad." Theodora laughed again. "Poor Luke; I would have said 'scoundrel.'"

"If you would rather be spending this brief hour with Arthur . . ."

"Of course I would rather be with Arthur. An educated man is always an enlivening companion."

"Cricket," Luke said. "Never would have thought we played cricket, would you?"

"Sing, sing," Theodora said, laughing.

Luke sang, in a nasal monotone, emphasizing each word distinctly:

"The first was young Miss Grattan,
She tried not to let him in;
He stabbed her with a corn knife,
That's how his crimes begin.

"The next was Grandma Grattan,
So old and tired and gray;
She fit off her attacker
Until her strength give way.

"The next was Grandpa Grattan,
A-settin' by the fire;
He crept up close behind him
And strangled him with a wire.

"The last was Baby Grattan
All in his trundle bed;
He stove him in the short ribs
Until that child was dead.

"And spit tobacco juice
All on his golden head."

When he finished there was a moment's silence, and then Theodora said weakly, "It's lovely, Luke. Perfectly beautiful. I will never hear it again without thinking of you."

"I plan to sing it to Arthur," Luke said. When are they going to talk about me? Eleanor wondered in the shadows. After a minute Luke went on idly, "I wonder what the doctor's book will be like, when he writes it? Do you suppose he'll put us in?"

"You will probably turn up as an earnest young psychic researcher. And I will be a lady of undeniable gifts but dubious reputation."

"I wonder if Mrs. Montague will have a chapter to herself."

"And Arthur. And Mrs. Dudley. I hope he doesn't reduce us all to figures on a graph."

"I wonder, I wonder," said Luke. "It's warm this afternoon," he said. "What could we do that is cool?"

"We could ask Mrs. Dudley to make lemonade."

"You know what I want to do?" Luke said. "I want to explore. Let's follow the brook up into the hills and see where it comes from; maybe there's a pond somewhere and we can go swimming."

"Or a waterfall; it looks like a brook that runs naturally from a waterfall."

"Come on, then." Listening behind the summerhouse, Eleanor heard their laughter and the sound of their feet running down the path to the house.

6

"Here's an interesting thing, here," Arthur's voice said in the manner of one endeavoring valiantly to entertain, "here in this book. Says how to make candles out of ordinary children's crayons."

"Interesting." The doctor sounded weary. "If you will excuse me, Arthur, I have all these notes to write up."

"Sure, Doctor. All got our work to do. Not a sound." Eleanor, listening outside the parlor door, heard the small irritating noises of Arthur settling down to be quiet. "Not much to do around here, is there?" Arthur said. "How d'you pass the time generally?"

"Working," the doctor said shortly.

"You writing down what happens in the house?"

"Yes."

"You got me in there?"

"No."

"Seems like you ought to put in our notes from planchette. What are you writing now?"

"Arthur. Can you read, or something?"

"Sure. Never meant to make a nuisance of myself." Eleanor heard Arthur take up a book, and put it down, and light a cigarette, and sigh, and stir, and finally say, "Listen, isn't there anything to *do* around here? Where *is* everybody?"

The doctor spoke patiently, but without interest. "Theodora and Luke have gone to explore the brook, I think. And I suppose the others are around somewhere. As a matter of fact, I believe my wife was looking for Mrs. Dudley."

"Oh." Arthur sighed again. "Might as well read, I guess," he said, and then, after a minute, "Say, Doctor. I don't like to bother you, but listen to what it says here in this book. . . ."

7

"No," Mrs. Montague said, "I do *not* believe in throwing young people together promiscuously, Mrs. Dudley. If my husband had consulted *me* before arranging this fantastic house party—"

"Well, now." It was Mrs. Dudley's voice, and Eleanor, pressed against the dining-room door, stared and opened her mouth wide against the wooden panels of the door. "I always say, Mrs. Montague, that you're only young once. Those young people are enjoying themselves, and it's only natural for the young."

"But living under one roof—"

"It's not as though they weren't grown up enough to know right from wrong. That pretty Theodora lady is old enough to take care of herself, I'd think, no matter how gay Mr. Luke."

"I need a dry dishtowel, Mrs. Dudley, for the silverware. It's a shame, I think, the way children grow up these days knowing everything. There should be more mysteries for them, more things that belong rightly to grownups, that they have to wait to find out."

"Then they find them out the hard way." Mrs. Dudley's voice was comfortable and easy. "Dudley brought in these tomatoes from the garden this morning," she said. "They did well this year."

"Shall I start on them?"

"No, oh, no. You sit down over there and rest; you've done enough. I'll put on the water and we'll have a nice cup of tea."

8

"Journeys end in lovers meeting," Luke said, and smiled across the room at Eleanor. "Does that blue dress on Theo really belong to you? I've never seen it before."

"I am Eleanor," Theodora said wickedly, "because I have a beard."

"You were wise to bring clothes for two," Luke told Eleanor. "Theo would never have looked half so well in my old blazer."

"I am Eleanor," Theo said, "because I am wearing blue. I love my love with an E because she is ethereal. Her name is Eleanor, and she lives in expectation."

She is being spiteful, Eleanor thought remotely; from a great distance, it seemed, she could watch these people and listen to them. Now she thought, Theo is being spiteful and Luke is trying to be nice; Luke is ashamed of himself for laughing at me and he is ashamed of Theo for being spiteful. "Luke," Theodora said, with a half-glance at Eleanor, "come and sing to me again."

"Later," Luke said uncomfortably. "The doctor has just set up the chessmen." He turned away in some haste.

Theodora, piqued, leaned her head against the back of her chair and closed her eyes, clearly determined not to speak. Eleanor sat, looking down at her hands, and listened to the sounds of the house. Somewhere upstairs a door swung quietly shut; a bird touched the tower briefly and flew off. In the kitchen the stove was settling and cooling, with little soft creakings. An animal—a rabbit?—moved through the bushes by the summerhouse. She could even hear, with her new awareness of the house, the dust drifting gently in the attics, the wood aging. Only the library was closed to her; she could not hear the heavy breathing of Mrs. Montague and Arthur over their planchette, nor their little excited questions; she could not hear the books rotting or rust seeping into the circular iron stairway to the tower. In the little parlor she could hear, without raising her eyes, Theodora's small irritated tappings and the quiet sound of the chessmen being set down. She heard when the library door slammed open, and then the sharp angry sound of footsteps coming to the little parlor, and then all of them turned as Mrs. Montague opened the door and marched in.

"I must say," said Mrs. Montague on a sharp, explosive breath, "I really must *say* that this is the most *infuriating*—"

"My dear." The doctor rose, but Mrs. Montague waved him aside angrily. "If you had the *decency*—" she said.

Arthur, coming behind her sheepishly, moved past her and, almost slinking, settled in a chair by the fire. He shook his head warily when Theodora turned to him.

"The common *decency*. After all, John, I *did* come all this way, and so did Arthur, just to help out, and I certainly must say that I never expected to meet with such cynicism and incredulity from *you*, of all people, and *these*—" She gestured at Eleanor and Theodora and Luke. "All I ask, all I *ask*, is some small minimum of trust, just a little bit of sympathy for all I am trying to do, and instead you disbelieve, you scoff, you mock and jeer." Breathing heavily, red-faced, she shook her finger at the doctor. "Planchette," she said bitterly, "will not speak to me tonight. Not *one single word* have I had from planchette, as a direct result of your sneering and your skepticism; planchette may very possibly not speak to me for a matter of weeks—it has happened before, I can tell you; it has happened before, when I subjected it to the taunts of unbelievers; I have known planchette to be silent for weeks, and the very *least* I could have expected, coming here as I did with none but the finest motives, was a little respect." She shook her finger at the doctor, wordless for the moment.

"My dear," the doctor said, "I am certain that none of us would knowingly have interfered."

"Mocking and jeering, were you not? Skeptical, with

planchette's very words before your eyes? Those young people pert and insolent?"

"Mrs. Montague, really . . ." said Luke, but Mrs. Montague brushed past him and sat herself down, her lips tight and her eyes blazing. The doctor sighed, started to speak, and then stopped. Turning away from his wife, he gestured Luke back to the chess table. Apprehensively, Luke followed, and Arthur, wriggling in his chair, said in a low voice to Theodora, "Never seen her so upset, you know. Miserable experience, waiting for planchette. So easily offended, of course. Sensitive to atmosphere." Seeming to believe that he had satisfactorily explained the situation, he sat back and smiled timidly.

Eleanor was hardly listening, wondering dimly at the movement in the room. Someone was walking around, she thought without interest; Luke was walking back and forth in the room, talking softly to himself; surely an odd way to play chess? Humming? Singing? Once or twice she almost made out a broken word, and then Luke spoke quietly; he was at the chess table where he belonged, and Eleanor turned and looked at the empty center of the room, where someone was walking and singing softly, and then she heard it clearly:

> Go walking through the valley,
> Go walking through the valley,
> Go walking through the valley,
> As we have done before. . . .

Why, I know that, she thought, listening, smiling, to the faint melody; we used to play that game; I remember that.

"It's simply that it's a most delicate and intricate piece of machinery," Mrs. Montague was saying to Theodora; she was still angry, but visibly softening under Theodora's sympathetic attention. "The slightest air of disbelief offends it, naturally. How would *you* feel if people refused to believe in *you?*"

> Go in and out the windows,
> Go in and out the windows,
> Go in and out the windows,
> As we have done before. . . .

The voice was light, perhaps only a child's voice, singing sweetly and thinly, on the barest breath, and Eleanor smiled and remembered, hearing the little song more clearly than Mrs. Montague's voice continuing about planchette.

> Go forth and face your lover,
> Go forth and face your lover,
> Go forth and face your lover,
> As we have done before. . . .

She heard the little melody fade, and felt the slight movement of air as the footsteps came close to her, and something almost brushed her face; perhaps there was a tiny sigh against her cheek, and she turned in surprise. Luke and the doctor bent over the chessboard, Arthur leaned confidingly close to Theodora, and Mrs. Montague talked.

None of them heard it, she thought with joy; nobody heard it but me.

〰〰〰〰〰〰〰〰〰〰〰〰〰〰〰〰〰〰〰〰〰〰

ELEANOR closed the bedroom door softly behind her, not wanting to awaken Theodora, although the noise of a door closing would hardly disturb anyone, she thought, who slept so soundly as Theodora; I learned to sleep very lightly, she told herself comfortingly, when I was listening for my mother. The hall was dim, lighted only by the small nightlight over the stairs, and all the doors were closed. Funny, Eleanor thought, going soundlessly in her bare feet along the hall carpet, it's the only house I ever knew where you don't have to worry about making noise at night, or at least about anyone knowing it's you. She had awakened with the thought of going down to the library, and her mind had supplied her with a reason: I cannot sleep, she explained to herself, and so I am going downstairs to get a book. If anyone asks me where I am going, it is down to the library to get a book because I cannot sleep.

It was warm, drowsily, luxuriously warm. She went barefoot and in silence down the great staircase and to the library door before she thought, But I can't go in there; I'm not allowed in there—and recoiled in the doorway before the odor of decay, which nauseated her. "Mother," she said aloud, and stepped quickly back. "Come along," a voice answered distinctly upstairs, and Eleanor turned, eager, and hurried to the staircase. "Mother?" she said softly, and then again, "Mother?" A little soft laugh floated down to her, and she ran, breathless, up the stairs and stopped at the top, looking to right and left along the hallway at the closed doors.

"You're here somewhere," she said, and down the hall the little echo went, slipping in a whisper on the tiny currents of air. "Somewhere," it said. "Somewhere."

Laughing, Eleanor followed, running soundlessly down the hall to the nursery doorway; the cold spot was gone, and she laughed up at the two grinning faces looking down at her. "Are you in here?" she whispered outside the door, "are you in here?" and knocked, pounding with her fists.

"Yes?" It was Mrs. Montague, inside, clearly just awakened. "Yes? Come in, whatever you are."

No, no, Eleanor thought, hugging herself and laughing silently, not in there, not with Mrs. Montague, and slipped away down the hall, hearing Mrs. Montague behind her calling, "I am your friend; I intend you no harm. Come in and tell me what is troubling you."

She won't open her door, Eleanor thought wisely; she is not afraid but she won't open her door, and knocked, pounding, against Arthur's door and heard Arthur's awakening gasp.

Dancing, the carpet soft under her feet, she came to the door behind which Theodora slept; faithless Theo, she thought, cruel, laughing Theo, wake up, wake up, wake up, and pounded and slapped the door, laughing, and shook the doorknob and then ran swiftly down the hall to Luke's door and pounded; wake up, she thought, wake up and be faithless. None of them will open their doors, she thought; they will sit inside, with the blankets pressed around them, shivering and wondering what is going to happen to them next; wake up, she thought, pounding on the doctor's door; I dare you to open your door and come out to see me dancing in the hall of Hill House.

Then Theodora startled her by calling out wildly, "Nell? Nell? Doctor, Luke, Nell's not here!"

Poor house, Eleanor thought, I had forgotten Eleanor; now they will have to open their doors, and she ran quickly down the stairs, hearing behind her the doctor's voice raised anxiously, and Theodora calling, "Nell? Eleanor?" What fools they are, she thought; now I will have to go into the library. "Mother, Mother," she whispered, "Mother," and stopped at the library door, sick. Behind her she could hear them talking upstairs in the hall; funny, she thought, I can feel the whole house, and heard even Mrs. Montague protesting, and Arthur, and then the doctor, clearly, "We've got to look for her; everyone please hurry."

Well, I can hurry too, she thought, and ran down the corridor to the little parlor, where the fire flickered briefly at her when she opened the door, and the chessmen sat where Luke and the doctor had left their game. The scarf Theodora had been wearing lay across the back of her chair; I can take care of *that* too, Eleanor thought, her maid's pathetic finery, and put one end of it between her teeth and pulled, tearing, and then dropped it when she heard them behind her on the stairs. They were coming down all together, anxious, telling one another where to look first, now and then calling, "Eleanor? Nell?"

"Coming? Coming?" she heard far away, somewhere else in the house, and she heard the stairs shake under their feet and a cricket stir on the lawn. Daring, gay, she ran down the corridor again to the hall and peeked out at them from the doorway. They were moving purposefully, all together, straining to stay near one another, and the doctor's flashlight swept the hall and stopped at the great front door, which was standing open wide. Then, in a rush, calling "Eleanor, *Eleanor*," they ran all together across the hall and out the front door, looking and calling, the flashlight moving busily. Eleanor clung to the door and laughed until tears came into her eyes; what fools they are, she thought; we trick them so easily. They are so slow, and so deaf and so *heavy*; they trample over the house, poking and peering and rough. She ran across the hall and through the game room and into the dining room and from there into the kitchen, with its doors. It's good here, she thought, I can go in any direction when I hear them. When they came back into the front hall, blundering and calling her, she darted quickly out onto the veranda into the cool night.

She stood with her back against the door, the little mists of Hill House curling around her ankles, and looked up at the pressing, heavy hills. Gathered comfortably into the hills, she thought, protected and warm; Hill House is lucky.

"Eleanor?" They were very close, and she ran along the veranda and darted into the drawing room; "Hugh Crain," she said, "will you come and dance with me?" She curtsied to the huge leaning statue, and its eyes flickered and shone at her; little reflected lights touched the figurines and the gilded chairs, and she danced gravely before Hugh Crain, who watched her, gleaming. "Go in and out the windows," she sang, and felt her hands taken as she danced. "Go in and out the windows," and she danced out onto the veranda and around the house. Going around and around and around the house, she thought, and none of them can see me. She touched a kitchen door as she passed, and six miles away Mrs. Dudley shuddered in her sleep. She came to the tower, held so tightly in the embrace of the house, in the straining grip of the house, and walked slowly past its gray stones, not allowed to touch even the outside. Then she turned and stood before the great doorway; the door was closed again, and she put out her hand and opened it effortlessly. Thus I enter Hill House, she told herself, and stepped inside as though it were her own. "Here I am," she said aloud. "I've been all around the house, in and out the windows, and I danced—"

"Eleanor?" It was Luke's voice, and she thought, Of all of them I would least like to have Luke catch me; don't let him see me, she thought beggingly, and turned and ran, without stopping, into the library.

And here I am, she thought. Here I am inside. It was not cold at all, but deliciously, fondly warm. It was light enough for her to see the iron stairway curving around and around up to the tower, and the little door at the top. Under her feet the stone floor moved caressingly, rubbing itself against the soles of her feet, and all around the soft air touched her, stirring her hair, drifting against her fingers, coming in a light breath across her mouth, and she danced in circles. No stone lions for me, she thought, no oleanders; I have broken the spell of Hill House and somehow come inside. I am home, she thought, and stopped in wonder at the thought. I am home, I am home, she thought; now to climb.

Climbing the narrow iron stairway was intoxicating—going higher and higher, around and around, looking down, clinging to the slim iron railing, looking far far down onto the stone floor. Climbing, looking down, she thought of the soft green grass outside and the rolling hills and the rich trees. Looking up, she thought of the tower of Hill House rising triumphantly between the trees, tall over the road which wound through Hillsdale and past a white house set in flowers and past the magic oleanders and past the stone lions and on, far, far away, to a little lady who was going to pray for her. Time is ended now, she thought, all *that* is gone and left behind, and that poor little lady, praying still, for me.

"Eleanor!"

For a minute she could not remember who they were (had they been guests of hers in the house of the stone lions? Dining at her long table in the candlelight? Had she met them at the inn, over the tumbling stream? Had one of them come riding down a green hill, banners flying? Had one of them run beside her in the darkness? and then she remembered, and they fell into place where they belonged) and she hesitated, clinging to the railing. They were so small, so ineffectual. They stood far below on the stone floor and pointed at her; they called to her, and their voices were urgent and far away.

"Luke," she said, remembering. They could hear her, because they were quiet when she spoke. "Doctor Montague," she said. "Mrs. Montague. Arthur." She could not remember the other, who stood silent and a little apart.

"Eleanor," Dr. Montague called, "turn around very carefully and come slowly down the steps. Move very, very slowly, Eleanor. Hold on to the railing all the time. Now turn and come down."

"What on earth is the creature doing?" Mrs. Montague demanded. Her hair was in curlers, and her bathrobe had a dragon on the stomach. "Make her come down so we can go back to bed. Arthur, make her come down at once."

"See here," Arthur began, and Luke moved to the foot of the stairway and started up.

"For God's sake be careful," the doctor said as Luke moved steadily on. "The thing is rotted away from the wall."

"It won't hold both of you," Mrs. Montague said positively. "You'll have it down on our heads. Arthur, move over here near the door."

"Eleanor," the doctor called, "can you turn around and start down slowly?"

Above her was only the little trapdoor leading out onto the turret; she stood on the little narrow platform at the top and pressed against the trapdoor, but it would not move. Futilely she hammered against it with her fists, thinking wildly, Make it open, make it open, or they'll catch me. Glancing over her shoulder, she could see Luke climbing steadily, around and around. "Eleanor," he said, "stand still. Don't move," and he sounded frightened.

I can't get away, she thought, and looked down; she saw one face clearly, and the name came into her mind. "Theodora," she said.

"Nell, do as they tell you. Please."

"Theodora? I can't get out; the door's been nailed shut."

"Damn right it's been nailed shut," Luke said. "And lucky for you, too, my girl." Climbing, coming very slowly, he had almost reached the narrow platform. "Stay perfectly still," he said.

"Stay perfectly still, Eleanor," the doctor said.

"Nell," Theodora said. "*Please* do what they say."

"Why?" Eleanor looked down and saw the dizzy fall of the tower below her, the iron stairway clinging to the tower walls, shaking and straining under Luke's feet, the cold stone floor, the distant, pale, staring faces. "How can I get down?" she asked helplessly. "Doctor—how can I get down?"

"Move very slowly," he said. "Do what Luke tells you."

"Nell," Theodora said, "don't be frightened. It will be all right, really."

"Of course it will be all right," Luke said grimly. "Probably it will only be *my* neck that gets broken. Hold on, Nell; I'm coming onto the platform. I want to get past you so you can go down ahead of me." He seemed hardly out of breath, in spite of climbing, but his hand trembled as he reached out to take hold of the railing, and his face was wet. "Come on," he said sharply.

Eleanor hung back. "The last time you told me to go ahead you never followed," she said.

"Perhaps I will just push you over the edge," Luke said. "Let you smash down there on the floor. Now behave yourself and move slowly; get past me and start down the stairs. And just hope," he added furiously, "that I can resist the temptation to give you a shove."

Meekly she came along the platform and pressed herself against the hard stone wall while Luke moved cautiously past her. "Start down," he said. "I'll be right behind you."

Precariously, the iron stairway shaking and groaning with every step, she felt her way. She looked at her hand on the railing, white because she was holding so tight, and at her bare feet going one at a time, step by step, moving with extreme care, but never looked down again to the stone floor. Go down very slowly, she told herself over and over, not thinking of more than the steps which seemed almost to bend and buckle beneath her feet, go down very very very slowly. "Steady," Luke said behind her. "Take it easy, Nell, nothing to be afraid of, we're almost there."

Involuntarily, below her, the doctor and Theodora held out their arms, as though ready to catch her if she fell, and once when Eleanor stumbled and missed a step, the handrail wavering as she clung to it, Theodora gasped and ran to hold the end of the stairway. "It's all right, my Nellie," she said over and over, "it's all right, it's all right."

"Only a little farther," the doctor said.

Creeping, Eleanor slid her feet down, one step after another, and at last, almost before she could believe it, stepped off onto the stone floor. Behind her the stairway rocked and clanged as Luke leaped down the last few steps and walked steadily across the room to fall against a chair and stop, head down and trembling still. Eleanor turned and looked up to the infinitely high little spot where she had been standing, at the iron stairway, warped and crooked and swaying against the tower wall, and said in a small voice, "I ran up. I ran up all the way."

Mrs. Montague moved purposefully forward from the doorway where she and Arthur had been sheltering against the probable collapse of the stairway. "Does anybody agree with me," she asked with great delicacy, "in thinking that this young woman has given us quite enough trouble to-night? *I*, for one, would like to go back to bed, and so would Arthur."

"Hill House—" the doctor began.

"This childish nonsense has almost certainly destroyed any chance of manifestations *tonight*, I can tell you. I certainly do not look to see any of our friends from beyond after *this* ridiculous performance, so if you will all excuse me—and if you are *sure* that you are finished with your posturing and performing and waking up busy people—I will say good night. Arthur." Mrs. Montague swept out, dragon rampant, quivering with indignation.

"Luke was scared," Eleanor said, looking at the doctor and at Theodora.

"Luke was most certainly scared," he agreed from behind her. "Luke was so scared he almost didn't get himself down from there. Nell, what an imbecile you are."

"I would be inclined to agree with Luke." The doctor

was displeased, and Eleanor looked away, looked at Theodora, and Theodora said, "I suppose you *had* to do it, Nell?"

"I'm all right," Eleanor said, and could not longer look at any of them. She looked, surprised, down at her own bare feet, realizing suddenly that they had carried her, unfeeling, down the iron stairway. She thought, looking at her feet, and then raised her head. "I came down to the library to get a book," she said.

2

It was humiliating, disastrous. Nothing was said at breakfast, and Eleanor was served coffee and eggs and rolls just like the others. She was allowed to linger over her coffee with the rest of them, observe the sunlight outside, comment upon the good day ahead; for a few minutes she might have been persuaded to believe that nothing had happened. Luke passed her the marmalade, Theodora smiled at her over Arthur's head, the doctor bade her good morning. Then, after breakfast, after Mrs. Dudley's entrance at ten, they came without comment, following one another silently, to the little parlor, and the doctor took his position before the fireplace. Theodora was wearing Eleanor's red sweater.

"Luke will bring your car around," the doctor said gently. In spite of what he was saying, his eyes were considerate and friendly. "Theodora will go up and pack for you."

Eleanor giggled. "She can't. She won't have anything to wear."

"Nell—" Theodora began, and stopped and glanced at Mrs. Montague, who shrugged her shoulders and said, "I examined the room. *Naturally*. I can't imagine why none of *you* thought to do it."

"I was going to," the doctor said apologetically. "But I thought—"

"You *always* think, John, and that's your trouble. *Naturally* I examined the room at once."

"Theodora's room?" Luke asked. "I wouldn't like to go in there again."

Mrs. Montague sounded surprised. "I can't think why not," she said. "There's nothing wrong with it."

"I went in and looked at my clothes," Theodora said to the doctor. "They're perfectly fine."

"The room needs dusting, *naturally*, but what can you expect if you lock the door and Mrs. Dudley cannot—"

The doctor's voice rose over his wife's. "—cannot tell you how sorry I am," he was saying. "If there is ever anything I can do . . ."

Eleanor laughed. "But I can't leave," she said, wondering where to find words to explain.

"You have been here quite long enough," the doctor said.

Theodora stared at her. "I don't need your clothes," she said patiently. "Didn't you just hear Mrs. Montague? I don't need your clothes, and even if I *did* I wouldn't wear them now; Nell, you've got to go away from here."

"But I can't leave," Eleanor said, laughing still because it was so perfectly impossible to explain.

"Madam," Luke said somberly, "you are no longer welcome as my guest."

"Perhaps Arthur *had* better drive her back to the city. Arthur could see that she gets there safely."

"Gets where?" Eleanor shook her head at them, feeling her lovely heavy hair around her face. "Gets where?" she asked happily.

"Why," the doctor said, "home, of course," and Theodora said, "Nell, your own little place, your own apartment, where all your things are," and Eleanor laughed.

"I haven't any apartment," she said to Theodora. "I made it up. I sleep on a cot at my sister's, in the baby's room. I haven't any home, no place at all. And I can't go back to my sister's because I stole her car." She laughed, hearing her own words, so inadequate and so unutterably sad. "I haven't any home," she said again, and regarded them hopefully. "No home. Everything in all the world that belongs to me is in a carton in the back of my car. That's all I have, some books and things I had when I was a little girl, and a watch my mother gave me. So you see there's no place you can send me."

I could, of course, go on and on, she wanted to tell them, seeing always their frightened, staring faces. I could go on and on, leaving my clothes for Theodora; I could go wandering and homeless, errant, and I would always come back here. It would be simpler to let me stay, more sensible, she wanted to tell them, happier.

"I want to stay here," she said to them.

"I've already spoken to the sister," Mrs. Montague said importantly. "I must say, she asked first about the car. A vulgar person; I told her she need have no fear. You were very wrong, John, to let her steal her sister's car and come here."

"My dear," Dr. Montague began, and stopped, spreading his hands helplessly.

"At any rate, she is expected. The sister was most annoyed at me because they had planned to go off on their vacation today, although why she should be annoyed at *me* . . ." Mrs. Montague scowled at Eleanor. "I do think someone ought to see her safely into their hands," she said.

The doctor shook his head. "It would be a mistake," he said slowly. "It would be a mistake to send one of us with her. She must be allowed to forget everything about this house as soon as she can; we cannot prolong the association. Once away from here, she will be herself again; can you find your way home?" he asked Eleanor, and Eleanor laughed.

"I'll go and get that packing done," Theodora said. "Luke, check her car and bring it around; she's only got one suitcase."

"Walled up alive." Eleanor began to laugh again at their stone faces. "Walled up alive," she said. "I want to stay here."

3

They made a solid line along the steps of Hill House, guarding the door. Beyond their heads she could see the windows looking down, and to one side the tower waited confidently. She might have cried if she could have thought of any way of telling them why; instead, she smiled brokenly up at the house, looking at her own window, at the amused, certain face of the house, watching her quietly. The house was waiting now, she thought, and it was waiting for her; no one else could satisfy it. "The house wants me to stay," she told the doctor, and he stared at her.

He was standing very stiff and with great dignity, as though he expected her to choose him instead of the house, as though, having brought her here, he thought that by unwinding his directions he could send her back again. His back was squarely turned to the house, and, looking at him honestly, she said, "I'm sorry. I'm terribly sorry, really."

"You'll go to Hillsdale," he said levelly; perhaps he was afraid of saying too much, perhaps he thought that a kind word, or a sympathetic one, might rebound upon himself and bring her back. The sun was shining on the hills and the house and the garden and the lawn and the trees and the brook; Eleanor took a deep breath and turned, seeing it all. "In Hillsdale turn onto Route Five going east; at Ashton you will meet Route Thirty-nine, and that will take you home. For your own safety," he added with a kind of urgency, "for your own safety, my dear; believe me, if I had foreseen this—"

"I'm really terribly sorry," she said.

"We can't take chances, you know, *any* chances. I am only beginning to perceive what a terrible risk I was asking of you all. Now . . ." He sighed and shook his head. "You'll remember?" he asked. "To Hillsdale, and then Route Five—"

"Look." Eleanor was quiet for a minute, wanting to tell them all exactly how it was. "I wasn't afraid," she said at last. "I really wasn't afraid. I'm fine now. I was—happy." She looked earnestly at the doctor. "*Happy*," she said. "I don't know what to say," she said, afraid again that she was going to cry. "I don't want to go away from here."

"There might be a next time," the doctor said sternly.

"Can't you understand that we *cannot* take that chance?"

Eleanor faltered. "Someone is praying for me," she said foolishly. "A lady I met a long time ago."

The doctor's voice was gentle, but he tapped his foot impatiently. "You will forget all of this quite soon," he said. "You must forget everything about Hill House. I was so wrong to bring you here," he said.

"How long *have* we been here?" Eleanor asked suddenly.

"A little over a week. Why?"

"It's the only time anything's ever happened to me. I liked it."

"That," said the doctor, "is why you are leaving in such a hurry."

Eleanor closed her eyes and sighed, feeling and hearing and smelling the house; a flowering bush beyond the kitchen was heavy with scent, and the water in the brook moved sparkling over the stones. Far away, upstairs, perhaps in the nursery, a little eddy of wind gathered itself and swept along the floor, carrying dust. In the library the iron stairway swayed, and light glittered on the marble eyes of Hugh Crain; Theodora's yellow shirt hung neat and unstained, Mrs. Dudley was setting the lunch table for five. Hill House watched, arrogant and patient. "I won't go away," Eleanor said up to the high windows.

"You *will* go away," the doctor said, showing his impatience at last. "Right now."

Eleanor laughed, and turned, holding out her hand. "Luke," she said, and he came toward her, silent. "Thank you for bringing me down last night," she said. "That was wrong of me. I know it now, and you were very brave."

"I was indeed," Luke said. "It was an act of courage far surpassing any other in *my* life. And I am glad to see you going, Nell, because I would certainly never do it again."

"Well, it seems to *me*," Mrs. Montague said, "if you're going you'd better get on with it. I've no quarrel with saying good-by, although I personally feel that you've all got an exaggerated view of this place, but I *do* think we've got better things to do than stand here arguing when we all know you've *got* to go. You'll be a time as it is, getting back to the city, and your sister waiting to go on her vacation."

Arthur nodded. "Tearful farewells," he said. "Don't hold with them, myself."

Far away, in the little parlor, the ash dropped softly in the fireplace. "John," Mrs. Montague said, "possibly it *would* be better if Arthur—"

"No," the doctor said strongly. "Eleanor has to go back the way she came."

"And who do I thank for a lovely time?" Eleanor asked.

The doctor took her by the arm and, with Luke beside her, led her to her car and opened the door for her. The carton was still on the back seat, her suitcase was on the floor, her coat and pocketbook on the seat; Luke had left the motor running. "Doctor," Eleanor said, clutching at him, "Doctor."

"I'm sorry," he said. "Good-by."

"Drive carefully," Luke said politely.

"You can't just *make* me go," she said wildly. "You *brought* me here."

"And I am sending you away," the doctor said. "We won't forget you, Eleanor. But right now the only important thing for *you* is to forget Hill House and all of us. Good-by."

"Good-by," Mrs. Montague said firmly from the steps, and Arthur said, "Good-by, have a good trip."

Then Eleanor, her hand on the door of the car, stopped and turned. "Theo?" she said inquiringly, and Theodora ran down the steps to her.

"I thought you weren't going to say good-by to me," she said. "Oh, Nellie, my Nell—be happy; please be happy. Don't *really* forget me; someday things really *will* be all right again, and you'll write me letters and I'll answer and we'll visit each other and we'll have fun talking over the crazy things we did and saw and heard in Hill House—oh, Nellie! I thought you weren't going to say good-by to me."

"Good-by," Eleanor said to her.

"Nellie," Theodora said timidly, and put out a hand to touch Eleanor's cheek, "listen—maybe someday we can meet here again? And have our picnic by the brook? We never had our picnic," she told the doctor, and he shook his head, looking at Eleanor.

"Good-by," Eleanor said to Mrs. Montague, "good-by, Arthur. Good-by, Doctor. I hope your book is very successful. Luke," she said, "good-by. And good-by."

"Nell," Theodora said, "please be careful."

"Good-by," Eleanor said, and slid into the car; it felt unfamiliar and awkward; I am too used already to the comforts of Hill House, she thought, and reminded herself to wave a hand from the car window. "Good-by," she called, wondering if there had ever been another word for her to say, "good-by, good-by." Clumsily, her hands fumbling, she released the brake and let the car move slowly.

They waved back at her dutifully, standing still, watching her. They will watch me down the drive as far as they can see, she thought; it is only civil for them to look at me until I am out of sight; so now I am going. Journeys end in lovers meeting. But I *won't* go, she thought, and laughed aloud to herself; Hill House is not as easy as *they* are; just by telling me to go away they can't make me leave, not if Hill House means me to stay. "Go away, Eleanor," she chanted aloud, "go away, Eleanor, we don't want you any more, not in *our* Hill House, go away, Eleanor, you can't stay *here*; but I can," she sang, "but I can; *they* don't make the rules around *here*. They can't turn me out or shut me out or laugh at me or hide from me; I won't go, and Hill House belongs to *me*."

With what she perceived as quick cleverness she pressed her foot down hard on the accelerator; they can't run fast enough to catch me this time, she thought, but by now they must be beginning to realize; I wonder who notices first? Luke, almost certainly. I can hear them calling now, she thought, and the little footsteps running through Hill House and the soft sound of the hills pressing closer. I am really doing it, she thought, turning the wheel to send the car directly at the great tree at the curve of the driveway, I am really doing it, I am doing this all by myself, now, at last; this is me, I am really really really doing it by myself.

In the unending, crashing second before the car hurled

into the tree she thought clearly, *Why* am I doing this? Why am I doing this? Why don't they stop me?

4

Mrs. Sanderson was enormously relieved to hear that Dr. Montague and his party had left Hill House; she would have turned them out, she told the family lawyer, if Dr. Montague had shown any sign of wanting to stay. Theodora's friend, mollified and contrite, was delighted to see Theodora back so soon; Luke took himself off to Paris, where his aunt fervently hoped he would stay for a while. Dr. Montague finally retired from active scholarly pursuits after the cool, almost contemptuous reception of his preliminary article analyzing the psychic phenomena of Hill House. Hill House itself, not sane, stood against its hills, holding darkness within; it had stood so for eighty years and might stand for eighty more. Within, its walls continued upright, bricks met neatly, floors were firm, and doors were sensibly shut; silence lay steadily against the wood and stone of Hill House, and whatever walked there, walked alone.

LIFE AMONG THE SAVAGES
Jackson's autobiography is crowded with the raucous voices of an extraordinary family living a wonderfully ordinary life.

> "Never before has the state of domestic chaos
> been so perfectly illuminated."
> —*The New York Times Book Review*

ISBN 0-14-026767-0

COME ALONG WITH ME
Along with Jackson's unfinished novel of the same title, this volume also contains sixteen short stories, including "The Lottery," and three of Jackson's lectures.

ISBN 0-14-025037-9

THE HAUNTING OF HILL HOUSE
Four seekers visit the abandoned Hill House mansion. At first their stay seems to be merely a spooky encounter with inexplicable noises and self-opening doors, but Hill House is gathering its powers and will soon choose one of them to make its own.

ISBN 0-14-007108-3

WE HAVE ALWAYS LIVED IN THE CASTLE
Merricat Blackwood, her sister Constance, and Uncle Julian live sequestered on the family estate after a fatal dose of arsenic kills most of their family. Their days pass in happy isolation until dangerous Cousin Charles appears.

> "A marvelous elucidation of life."
> —*The New York Times Book Review*

ISBN 0-14-007107-5

In every corner of the world, on every subject under the sun, Penguin represents quality and variety—the very best in publishing today.

For complete information about books available from Penguin—including Puffins, Penguin Classics, and Arkana—and how to order them, write to us at the appropriate address below. Please note that for copyright reasons the selection of books varies from country to country.

In the United Kingdom: Please write to *Dept. EP, Penguin Books Ltd, Bath Road, Harmondsworth, West Drayton, Middlesex UB7 0DA.*

In the United States: Please write to *Penguin Putnam Inc., P.O. Box 12289 Dept. B, Newark, New Jersey 07101-5289* or call 1-800-788-6262.

In Canada: Please write to *Penguin Books Canada Ltd, 10 Alcorn Avenue, Suite 300, Toronto, Ontario M4V 3B2.*

In Australia: Please write to *Penguin Books Australia Ltd, P.O. Box 257, Ringwood, Victoria 3134.*

In New Zealand: Please write to *Penguin Books (NZ) Ltd, Private Bag 102902, North Shore Mail Centre, Auckland 10.*

In India: Please write to *Penguin Books India Pvt Ltd, 11 Panchsheel Shopping Centre, Panchsheel Park, New Delhi 110 017.*

In the Netherlands: Please write to *Penguin Books Netherlands bv, Postbus 3507, NL-1001 AH Amsterdam.*

In Germany: Please write to *Penguin Books Deutschland GmbH, Metzlerstrasse 26, 60594 Frankfurt am Main.*

In Spain: Please write to *Penguin Books S. A., Bravo Murillo 19, 1° B, 28015 Madrid.*

In Italy: Please write to *Penguin Italia s.r.l., Via Benedetto Croce 2, 20094 Corsico, Milano.*

In France: Please write to *Penguin France, Le Carré Wilson, 62 rue Benjamin Baillaud, 31500 Toulouse.*

In Japan: Please write to *Penguin Books Japan Ltd, Kaneko Building, 2-3-25 Koraku, Bunkyo-Ku, Tokyo 112.*

In South Africa: Please write to *Penguin Books South Africa (Pty) Ltd, Private Bag X14, Parkview, 2122 Johannesburg.*